PATRICIA WILSON

dangerous obsession

Harlequin Books

TORONTO • NEW YORK • LONDON
AMSTERDAM • PARIS • SYDNEY • HAMBURG
STOCKHOLM • ATHENS • TOKYO • MILAN

Harlequin Presents first edition July 1990
ISBN 0-373-11286-6

Original hardcover edition published in 1989
by Mills & Boon Limited

CHAPTER ONE

IT WOULD rain soon. Anna knew it, but she still kept on walking through the woods. There was something about walking that eased the mind, or so they said. Nothing could ease her mind at the moment. She looked up into the trees, giant trees, old trees; they had been in this parkland for centuries and seen so many changes, so many people who had lived and died at Langford Hall. Not one of them could have been more loved than Gavin Toren. She had loved him like a father and his sudden death had left her shattered. She was not a Toren, she was Anna Mazzini and she had always known that. In spite of the love and care that Gavin had shown her, in spite of her deep love and friendship for Elaine, she had never been in any doubt that she was merely Gavin's ward and no Toren at all. Dan had seen to that!

Soon, very soon, Dan would arrive. It irritated her that she would have to bow to any decision he made, but for now there was nothing she could do. He would soon know about the plans for her future, and if he felt as annoyed as she did then everything was going to be all right. In any case, there was trouble enough, and she didn't want Elaine brought into any further distress. For once in his life, Dan would have to listen to her.

She hadn't seen him for four years, not since she was nearly eighteen and just accepted at Oxford. Maybe he was no longer the same. Perhaps he didn't care about Elaine either now? Perhaps he would want to sell

Langford Hall? The new responsibility that had been thrust upon him would make him furious. Well, she would have to face that. He wouldn't be the only one who was furious!

The sky was almost black with the threatening rain as she came to the edge of the woods and faced Langford Hall across the wide expanse of lawn. It always brought a queer tilt to her heart to see the clean, beautifully balanced lines of the old Georgian mansion, and this time she looked at it more closely than ever. Soon, perhaps, she would never see it again. It all depended upon what Dan decided to do. All her hopes and fears had once been wrapped up in this house, all her childish dreams.

She took a deep breath and stepped out for the house. Wallowing in self-pity was not really her style. Elaine had more than enough to worry about without comforting her. She entered the large, square hall, turning at once to the drawing-room at the sound of voices. It wasn't Dan. He hadn't yet arrived, and she knew that for sure because the only car parked at the front was her own Polo, a present from Gavin on her twenty-first birthday four months ago. Tears misted her dark eyes. She would never see Gavin Toren again. She was on her own finally.

And what would Dan say? They hadn't even been able to get in touch with him to give him time to get here for the funeral. He would be three days late. He would never see his father again. Would he blame them? Would he be bitter? No, not Dan! Dan would just arrive and take over. If he had bothered to come home more often, then he would have seen his father before the end. His coming now would only tie up a few loose ends. Elaine waited for him as if he could solve any problem at all, and he

probably could, for Elaine. To Anna he meant trouble, unless he was utterly indifferent and saw her as merely a nuisance. That would be nothing unusual!

'Dan's going to arrive in the middle of a rain storm!'

Elaine looked up and spoke as Anna came into the room, her voice calm whatever she was feeling. She was curled up on the settee, looking weary and worried, and Anna squashed her own worries at the sight of Elaine's pale face.

'Maybe he won't come until tomorrow?'

Edna, the Toren housekeeper, was obviously the one who had been talking to Elaine, but Anna shook her head as Edna voiced this thought.

'He'll come soon, tonight!'

Elaine smiled, her weary face brightening for a moment as she looked across at Anna.

'You've always known when Dan would be here. I've always thought that uncanny. Maybe it's the Welsh blood in you on your mother's side.'

Maybe it's because I've always had to watch my step with Dan, and developed an instinct to warn me, Anna thought bitterly. She only smiled, though, and Edna bustled out of the room.

Elaine's eyes lingered on Anna's face. She was always a brilliant picture to look at, jet-black hair straight and long, hanging down her back like a thick curtain that invariably gleamed with blue lights. Dark eyes, thick-lashed, and a beautiful skin that was faintly olive-tinted, soft rose-tinged at her cheeks. Her bright red woollen jacket vied with her brilliant colour but lost, and Elaine's eyes stayed on her. Anna had always been secret and dark and, in spite of their great affection for each other, Elaine always felt slightly immature at the side of her,

although she was nearly four years older. Perhaps it was all that striking darkness? Perhaps it was the Italian blood and the Welsh blood that made Anna a very complex character. It was probably just that Anna was brilliantly clever!

'What's Dan going to say?' Elaine asked anxiously. 'I've no idea what to do about the wedding! It will be so difficult to postpone. I don't think I could face the extra organisation. I've spoken to Uncle Jack and he's willing to take Dad's place and give me away. Will Dan object, though? It's only two weeks from now, and he won't even have time to get used to being home, to not having Dad around.'

'I'm sure he won't object!' Anna said with more conviction than she felt. Who knew what Dan would say? Who knew what he was thinking? He would get a succession of shocks as soon as he arrived. His father had died suddenly, Elaine's wedding was already arranged, the invitations sent out, and then there was this guardian business.

Lurking at the back of her mind was the problem of her finals, but the back of her mind was where it would have to stay for now. After she had helped Elaine to fight any battle with Dan, she would feel able to get on with her revision. About the other thing, Dan would be in agreement with her for once, she was sure. Her guardian was dead and, at twenty-one, she didn't need another, and certainly not Dan. He would not want to be burdened; his life was too fast and furious, too glamorous. Even so, she was a bit nervous, gearing herself up for an imaginary fight, anxious about him, as she had been all her life in this house.

The phone rang and it was Steve, wanting Elaine. Anna thought it a good opportunity to go out of the room. She was thinking too much to keep her face expressionless, and as the subject of her thoughts was Dan it was as well to escape. Her face had been schooled for years to show no emotion when Dan was there, but she might slip.

'Shall I serve afternoon tea now, or wait for Mr Toren to arrive?' Edna stuck her head into the room and looked questioningly at Anna.

'We'll wait a little longer, I don't think either of us is desperate. I've got a few things to sort out in my room!'

She stood quickly, glad of the excuse to get out and be alone. It was difficult to sit there with Elaine's eyes scanning her face, wondering as she wondered herself how Dan would react to everything.

'That brother of yours is going to be late!' Edna informed her as she stepped into the hall and made for the big, dark oak staircase and the tranquillity of her room.

'He's not coming from just up the road! He's coming from California. I think we can allow him a little extra time. In any case, he'll be here soon. Keep the kettle boiling.' Anna managed a slight smile. He was not *her* brother! He had made that plain in so many ways, ever since her childhood.

Edna's face looked satisfied, years of knowledge of the family in her next words.

'That's all right, then. You were always close to Mr Dan!'

Not likely! It was just that she had always known which side her bread was buttered on, how to keep her head out of the lion's mouth! Anna turned and raced

up the stairs, facing facts squarely. She was worried. It was no use denying it. Dan had always had a great deal of power over her. He had been eighteen when she had arrived at this house, Elaine ten, and the two girls had got on famously. Dan of course was older, and not much given to carting two younger girls around with him, but even as she was growing up he had been toweringly domineering, or so it seemed, although he never criticised her openly. It was there in his eyes, though. Would he wish to go on as before, ignoring her for most of the time, or would he now wish to interfere?

Well, there was no escape, she couldn't simply cut and run, plead the need to go back to Oxford. It was the end of term and she couldn't think of one good reason to go back yet, except to escape from Dan. Elaine needed her, in any case, and she was no coward. She was used to facing things.

Thankfully she closed her door, although it didn't really help except that now nobody could see her face. There was nothing to do here, and she walked across to the window, looking down at the front of the house, not switching on the light, waiting for Dan to arrive. That was nothing new! She had waited for him to arrive for most of her life, wondering how he would be. When he was at Cambridge she had awaited his holidays with trepidation, praying that Gavin wouldn't begin to boast again about her school results. He always had, and Dan would look at her with those tawny eyes until she became all anxious and trembling.

Once, Dan had picked her up and given her a hug, and she had been so shocked by any show of affection from him that she had wriggled with fright until he put her down. He had been highly amused, so had Gavin.

Dan had called her a 'prickly little hedgehog'. But she had always known that it was necessary to hide the fact that almost everything she did was to please Dan, that she wanted his interest, his approval. He was utterly indifferent for most of the time.

She closed her mind to the past and forced herself to remember that Dan would be tired, grief-stricken, probably in need of help himself; while Elaine waited for him as if he was the answer to all things, and she waited with selfish fears racing around in the back of her mind. It was Dan's father who had died so suddenly. She must try to be normal and give him no other cause for grief.

There was nothing very normal about standing staring out at the darkening landscape, but she was still doing that when the car came up the long drive. She didn't recognise it. She was still so far back in the past, expecting Dan's Porsche. Of course he would have hired a car at the airport. It had to be Dan. She could feel it.

When he stopped and stepped out, she drew back behind the curtain, even though it was probably too dark for her to be seen anyway, certainly too dark from down there. She could see him, though, and her heart gave a queer lurch as he got out and straightened up. Had she expected him to have changed? He had not, not from here.

The lights from the house caught his hair, the dark golden-bronze colour of it that was so perfect with those clear tawny eyes. He was in a dark suit, the white of his shirt startlingly clear from here, almost as if she could reach down and touch him. How many times in her life had she seen Dan arrive? How many times had she

watched anxiously from here? It was like looking at her past life in one searing flash.

He stood looking across the parkland, out towards the woods, and then turned to the house, his eyes running over it almost lovingly. He too was remembering his life in this house before fame and necessity had taken him away. He raised his head and his eyes moved upwards, straight to her window, and Anna gasped, drawing back even more. He couldn't see her! Surely he couldn't see even a vague glimpse in this light? It was sheer chance that his eyes had moved straight to her room. And what was she doing behaving like this? There was nothing natural about her, even though she had been determined to show that she had forgotten the way they had always skirted carefully around each other. She should have waved, opened the window and called down!

She heard the car door slam and knew she could not put off the meeting for much longer. Dan was home. He had to be greeted. His father was dead and he would expect to see Elaine and herself at once. He had to be helped with his grief. Her battle with him, if there was to be one, would come later.

She glanced at herself in the mirror, hastily running a comb through her thick, long hair. Perhaps she should have changed? This red jacket was hardly suitable at a time like this, and she was wearing jeans, her college 'uniform'. It was too late now. If she delayed, he would think she was avoiding him. He knew she had good reason to avoid him. She went out of her room and along the passage to the stairs.

She could hear them in the hall even before she reached the top of the staircase.

'Dan, we couldn't get in touch with you in time. We rang Nassau and asked them to send a launch to the island, but they already knew you weren't there!'

'It's all right, Elaine. It was all so sudden, wasn't it? I had to be away. They're filming the final sequence of my latest book, there were a few alterations to the script. I went there with the firm intention of coming straight on to England for your wedding. I never expected that...' The rich, deep voice stopped suddenly and then picked up. 'Anyway, I was finished and ready to leave when I finally got the message from you.'

Elaine flung her arms around his neck.

'I'm so sorry, Dan. I wish you could have been here. It's been so terrible!' Everything hurt Elaine deeply, and Dan smiled, gathering his sister close, his face against her hair.

'I know, honey. I know,' he murmured softly, more comforting than comforted. Anna was half-way down the stairs when he saw her, and he went on holding Elaine, his eyes on Anna as she moved down into the hall. He must have stiffened, because Elaine suddenly drew back and looked up, seeing Anna too.

'Hello, Dan.' She couldn't think of anything else to say. Seeing him again was a bigger shock than she had bargained for, and Elaine had said they were sorry, had explained why he was not able to be contacted before the funeral. He had to know that she was sorry, too. She had loved Gavin Toren like a father. He was the only father she remembered. Surely Dan knew that? It was not Elaine who had tried to contact Dan, she had done that. Elaine had gone to pieces.

'Anna.' He just said her name in that softly deep voice, and she was standing in front of him as he moved

forward to meet her. He didn't clasp her close, though, as he had done with Elaine, and she was grateful for that; she hadn't quite got her act together but it would come. His hands came to her shoulders and he just looked down at her.

He was just the same, except that he seemed more tanned than ever. His golden-bronze hair gleamed in the lights, the same well-cut thick hair framing the handsome face, his hazel eyes tawny above the high cheekbones. They were slightly long eyes, heavily lashed, almost beautiful. There was no softness in his face, though. It was strong and filled with character, probably too much character. It could be a dangerous face.

Almost stealthily her eyes moved over him, seeing the fine-drawn lines of weariness, the tired look of that firm mouth, the sleepless glaze to his eyes.

'You're tired!' It sounded almost accusing, and for the first time the carved lips quirked into a slight smile.

'I apologise.' His eyes gleamed momentarily with the old remembered derisive laughter, and she looked away abruptly, suddenly unbearably conscious of those strong hands on her slender shoulders, other memories making her withdraw a little.

'I'll miss him, Dan!' she whispered, grief-stricken all over again, and he suddenly drew her close in a loose embrace.

'I know,' he sighed, his hands running down the shining length of her hair.

'I'll serve dinner now. It's too late for afternoon tea!'

Edna's appearance and her stubborn look jerked them all out of a sort of timeless trance, and Dan straightened, releasing Anna and turning to his luggage that stood in the hall by the door.

'Give me ten minutes, Edna,' he ordered quietly. 'I'll just have a quick freshen up.'

'Yes, Mr Toren!' Edna's pouting look vanished. Dan was back and she knew now that the ship had a strong hand at the helm. He gave her a quick peck on the cheek as he passed, and she disappeared into the kitchen as rosy as an apple.

They were all family again, except that Gavin was missing. As they sat in the drawing-room after dinner, Anna kept well into the background and watched. She had always done that when Dan was there, and she slipped into her old role easily. Dan had eased Elaine's worries, calmed her. His very presence was a comfort in an odd sort of way, because even though Anna knew that her turn would come, that those tawny eyes would finally get around to her, probing and questioning; it felt as if he had never been away, as their problems were brought out and aired.

'Steve and I...well—we'll postpone the wedding,' Elaine offered nervously, but Dan's eyes were on her at once, his strong face softened.

'Don't!' He smiled as if his swift word had been harsh and as if he wanted to make sure she didn't feel upset. 'It's two weeks. The arrangements have all been made. Keep it like that, Elaine. Dad would have wanted it.'

'I—I don't know, Dan...'

'I do,' he assured her softly. 'Life goes on, Elaine. You loved him while he was here. Live your life now.'

'What about giving the bride away, Dan? I thought perhaps Uncle Jack...'

'I agree!' His hands covered Elaine's. 'I'm glad you didn't pass that on to me! I wouldn't have liked to stand in for Dad.'

He looked unbearably sad for a moment, and then his gaze turned to Anna, his eyes very intent.

'What do you plan to do?'

'After the finals?' Anna glanced across at him. 'I'll stay on in Oxford, get a temporary job until the results are out. Maybe I'll go to Wales and visit my home country—or Italy, that's my home country, too. In any case, Elaine will be married and in her own home. This is your house. Langford Hall has been in your family for generations.'

His brows had drawn together as she mentioned a temporary job, but at her last words he looked really angry, his lips tightening.

'Since you became Gavin's ward, this has been your home. It's still your home! I don't know what the Will says and I don't much care! I've made all the money already that I'm ever going to need. I don't live here, and I don't plan to live here! If you think that...'

'I'm not suggesting you would think of throwing me out!' Anna looked away from his suddenly tight face. 'Gavin and I talked things over long ago. He knew that if he ever—died, I'd go... I couldn't...'

She stopped, too choked with tears to continue, and he took pity on her, leaving her future to some other time. It boded ill for the immediate future. He didn't know yet. Elaine didn't know, either. Maybe the solicitor wouldn't tell Dan? Maybe Gavin hadn't meant it? After all, he had been very ill.

'It's your final term,' Dan suddenly said, his tawny eyes keenly on her composed face.

'Yes.' She was fiercely glad that she had her emotions well under control at once. It wasn't easy, facing that intent look; memories kept intruding, and she hadn't quite got used to him again. She was beginning to realise just how short a time four years really was.

'So then what?' His lips quirked at her brief answer, and she felt colour mounting under her skin. She had always been brief in replies when she was disturbed, either brief or turbulent, swinging from one extreme to the other.

'I haven't quite decided yet. When I get my finals out of the way, I'll see what turns up. I'm more or less determined to go overseas.'

'Determined? That's an odd choice of word!' One dark eyebrow raised and he kept his gaze punishingly on her face. 'It has nothing to do with the fact that you'll feel homeless?'

'Nothing at all! I always intended that. Gavin knew and so does Elaine. Of course,' she added softly, 'I might fail my finals.'

'It's not very likely, is it?' Dan murmured mockingly. 'You've sailed through so far.'

'How do you...?'

'Dad. We communicated!' he assured her drily. 'Straight maths! What the hell are you going to do with that?'

'There are endless possibilities,' Anna said a little tightly. 'I could go into industry, the banking world, the government...' He was being scathing again, just as he had always been.

He was suddenly laughing softly. 'Government? I'm glad I live overseas. When you lose that prickly temper, the repercussions will be felt worldwide.'

'It may even reach you in your island paradise!' She wished she hadn't said that as soon as the words left her mouth, because Dan caught the touch of bitterness in her tone and his hazel eyes narrowed.

'I don't think so,' he assured her with a wry look. 'Owning an island, however small, has certain advantages. I have all the necessary equipment for survival, and endless peace. That's why I've lived there these past four years. I can get on with writing.'

And be alone with my wife! He didn't say that, but it was there, on his face, and Anna looked away abruptly, her eyes turned to the crackling fire.

'Oh, Dan, we've never asked about Daphne! How is she?'

'Very well,' Dan said in an unruffled voice. 'The baby is three now. Daphne decided to call him Trevor.'

Every word cut into Anna like a knife, taking her by surprise. She was over it. Better. Dan was back into the niche he had always occupied. Even so, she wanted to escape. She was just wondering rather desperately how she was going to manage it when Edna put her head around the door.

'Telephone, Miss Anna. It's from Oxford.'

'You're being recalled?' Dan asked sardonically, and she flashed him a look that was quite impatient, in spite of the fact that he was only just home. He could be quite patronising sometimes. He usually was!

'I'm not in the government yet! It's almost certain to be Bryan,' she added with a brilliant glance at Elaine, sickened with herself for this desire to put on an act, to gush. She had nothing to prove to Dan.

'Bryan?' She heard Dan's murmured question as she raced out of the room, eagerness in every movement.

'Anna's boyfriend,' Elaine confided in a low voice. 'I would have thought Dad had told you. There may be other wedding bells soon!'

Anna closed the door into the hall and leaned against it momentarily, her eyes closed, her breathing unsteady. Bless Bryan for getting her out of there. If she went on like this, there would soon be an atmosphere.

'Are you all right?'

Edna was standing holding the phone as she normally did, certain in her own mind that if she rested it on the table for more than a second the line would go dead.

'I'm fine! Give me a minute and then put it down. I'll take it in the study.' Anna pulled herself together and went across the hall. She would have to watch her step. If Dan ever saw her like that, he would instantly think...

'What's happening up there? I hope you're not getting too miserable, Anna? No amount of misery will bring Gavin Toren back.' Bryan's voice was so welcome, and he prided himself on sound practical advice. It was only because he was worried about her.

'I'm all right,' she assured him. 'In any case, Dan's here now!'

What was she saying? It would have been much more all right if Dan had never come. Somehow they would have managed. They had managed for long enough! But Gavin had been there then, she reminded herself. *She* could manage, but Elaine never could, not until she was safely in Steve's keeping.

'Ah, the famous brother!'

There it was again! For a second she felt angry with Bryan.

'I'm not related to anyone,' she reminded him a little sharply. 'Elaine is Dan's sister. I'm nothing at all!'

'Sorry! Did I hit a raw spot there?'

'No!' Anna forced a laugh. 'It's just that your mistake is the second time tonight. Edna said that earlier.'

'And did you go down her throat?' he enquired in amusement. 'I thought you had been brought up as one family?'

'We have. Will you stop prying into my life?' She was laughing, and he let the matter drop, to her great relief. What she was to Dan was not a subject she wished to probe at the moment. She turned Bryan's mind to other things. It was nice to have a gossip with him.

CHAPTER TWO

THEY were both talking quietly when she went back, and Dan never even glanced around.

'Is it all fixed, then, Anna?' Elaine smiled across at her. 'Has Bryan arranged to get away for the wedding?'

'No. I'm sorry, Elaine. The hospital is so understaffed that he can't get even that day off.'

'He's a doctor,' Elaine explained to Dan. 'He did his finals last year, and now he's doing his time in a hospital. Oh, that sounds like Dartmoor! Sorry, Anna!' Elaine laughed. 'It's all right about him not coming. Just don't try to back out of being chief bridesmaid.'

'As if I would!' She was suddenly aware of Dan's eyes on her again, although he had no comment to make, and she hastily added, 'I'll go and help Edna with the dishes, I think.'

'I'm not offering,' Elaine said firmly, and Anna shot her a smile.

'Just sit there and grow beautiful!'

'If I could grow as beautiful as you, I'd sit still for months,' Elaine assured her.

'Flattery? You must be wanting something.'

'Will you come with me to the shops tomorrow?' Elaine asked in her most wheedling voice.

'You mean, will I *drive* you to the shops tomorrow,' Anna corrected. 'The answer is yes, providing you get out of bed before seven!'

She turned to the door, but Dan's voice stopped her.

'You're still an early riser, then?'

'Now and always!' Anna retorted, drifting out of the room. Even the sound of his voice made her feel strange, a resentment inside her still. It was ridiculous! He was married! He didn't even know about the burden that had been wished on him. He certainly wouldn't want it. She attacked the dishes with gusto, until Edna protested that she would rather have had no help and kept her nerves intact. Anna wasn't really listening, though. Her thoughts were trying to fly away from her, to take their own well-trodden path, but she refused to let them. The past was long ago forgotten. The future would be tricky enough after tomorrow...

Dan was alone when she went back into the drawing-room, and she absolutely refused to back out stealthily. She wouldn't have had the chance, in any case, because he turned swiftly at the sound of the door opening. He was flicking water from his jacket, and she stared as if she had an unnatural interest in this action.

'You're wet!'

It was a stupid thing to say, but it covered a moment of unease. She looked round the room as if she was hoping that Elaine was hiding, and as usual her nervous way with him irritated him at once.

'She went to bed,' Dan informed her tersely. 'I'm wet because it's still raining heavily. I went to put the car away. Does that cover all the points?'

'Did you?' She knew she was just staring at him, getting used to him again, and for a moment he looked impatient.

'Did I what? Put the car away? No! I was blocked by a white Polo. It seems to have been abandoned by the front door!'

'Oh, I'm sorry. If you'd told me...'

'It's yours?' He leaned against the mantelpiece, his hands in his pockets now, and regarded her steadily.

'Yes. Your father gave it to me for my twenty-first birthday.'

'Four months ago,' Dan surprised her by saying. She was astounded that he even knew she was still alive. She wanted to go now, but he still wanted to talk.

'Don't you ever intend to come back here at all?' he suddenly shot at her.

'I haven't thought about it,' she lied, moving to the window and looking out at the dark, rainy night. 'Right now my mind has too much to cope with. There was the thought of Elaine's marriage, the finals and then—then...'

'It must have been a great shock to you, Anna,' Dan said softly. 'You were only just seven when you came here to Langford Hall. Dad was always like a father to you. I wish I could have been here!'

'We tried to get in touch with you,' she said hastily, but he wasn't being angry anyway.

'You mean *you* tried to get in touch with me,' he corrected. 'I know Elaine too well. She just falls apart in any crisis. She doesn't have your composure.'

'We never even suspected that his heart...' Anna said quickly. Praise from Dan, if that was what it was, was so scarce as to be frightening. She made herself turn to face him and say what had been on her mind for every miserable minute since Gavin's death. 'You won't sell Langford Hall, will you, Dan? You're rich! You'll never

need the money. I couldn't bear to think of anyone else...'

'No,' he assured her softly. 'I'll never sell. It holds too many memories. I'm surprised that you feel so strongly about the place, as you're determined to leave it. You were never quite settled here, were you?'

'I loved Gavin,' she said with a stubbornness to cover hurt. Maybe she would have been settled if Dan had been different.

'He loved you. Your mother chose well when she asked Dad to be your guardian.'

'They were very, very distant relatives!'

'And he was once deeply in love with her, until a dark and handsome Italian came along,' Dan said quietly.

'You're joking! How can you possibly say that?' She looked at him in astonishment, but his lips quirked with amusement, the tawny eyes intently on her face.

'Dad told me. That's why he agreed to have you here. That's why he loved you so much.'

'And not for myself at all?' Anna asked bitterly, hurt, although she knew exactly what to expect from Dan.

'I didn't mean that. If I implied it, then I'm sorry,' he assured her irritably. 'You know perfectly well that he loved you for yourself!'

'Even though I'm a strange oddity.' Anna's tongue seemed to have taken on a bitter life of its own.

'He never seemed to notice,' Dan informed her drily. 'I wonder how the Will is going to cope with the fact that your parents insisted that you have a guardian until you were twenty-five?' he added thoughtfully. 'I don't know how the law stands there. Maybe you'll inherit your legacy straight away?'

She almost shot out of the room, leaving him to think whatever he chose. She couldn't stand there and lie to him about it. She couldn't tell him, either, that he seemed to have been landed with the task. The solicitor had only spoken to her about her own affairs. Gavin had set her up as a separate client with his own solicitor, who had written to her as soon as he knew that Gavin had died. She was disgusted with herself that she hadn't had the courage to tell him at once, to get it all over with! She was still wary of Dan.

She had secretly idolised him ever since she had come to this house. His laughing eyes seemed to be everywhere, and her happiness was out of all proportion to the deed when those eyes smiled at her. It was difficult to keep them smiling as she got bigger and began to have her own opinions and her own friends. Dan could be very caustic if he disapproved of anything.

She sighed, wishing she had already taken her finals and that, like Bryan, she was too tied to a job to be here any longer than tomorrow. She could have come to Elaine's wedding, faced things for the one day. Would Dan stay here all the time? Why hadn't he brought Daphne with him? Maybe the misery of a house that had just lost a loved one was not a suitable place for a child. She closed her door and locked it, but the thought of sleep was never more far away.

She showered and changed for bed, sitting at the mirror to brush her long shining hair, her eyes looking blankly back at her. She hadn't always looked like this. She knew she had changed four years ago, changed suddenly, her quick swing of character inexplicable to Gavin and Elaine. They had put it down to college and hard work, but it wasn't that at all. Things had always come

easily to her, and she had always worked hard at school; everything she did was for Dan. Her days spent trying to please him.

She was a madcap, almost wild, but she never crossed Dan. She could never have faced a reprimand from him. Her hair had been long, a thick braid down to the bottom of her back, and she had been painfully thin, feeling awkward and ugly when Elaine, almost four years older, had begun to blossom out.

'How you can look so wild and be so clever at school is a mystery. It must be some sort of trick, witchcraft!' Gavin used to say. But he had been amusedly proud when she had taken prize after prize. Dan never said anything. She wasn't sure if he even knew.

Then suddenly Dan was famous, the exciting books he wrote best sellers, being filmed, and he wasn't there any more. She had always been subdued when he was at home, but it was enough that he had been there, that she could see him, even though he had looked at her oddly from time to time, as if he thought she was strange. The looks had usually ended with a wide, infectious smile, though, and it was all worth it, although she had no idea how to get close to him. She would not have dared.

She had been fourteen when he'd gone to America to write the screenplay for his first book to be filmed, and she could hardly grasp the fact that he would be away almost permanently. He was twenty-five, and of course he had been away before. She had always been unhappily withdrawn when he'd gone, but he had come back often. And when he'd begun to write he had stayed at Langford Hall. It didn't matter that he never noticed

her except to keep her strictly in line. He was there and nothing else mattered.

'He's coming back, you know!'

Gavin had found her crying silently after he had gone, and she knew that she was too obsessed with Dan, that he was grown up and busy, but somehow she couldn't help it.

He didn't come back for three years, and suddenly his letters stopped too. She worked madly, more to occupy her time than for any other reason, and when he did come she was seventeen, and had just heard that she had a place at Oxford because of her exam results.

Anna got up and walked to the window, looking down at the front of the house at the two cars glittering in the rain, hers and Dan's. She had been here when he'd come back. She was too excited, too shy suddenly to just wait with everyone else, but the excitement died on her face as he got out of the car and came round to help the woman out.

She was beautiful, Dan's age, slender and fair, almost fragile, and even from above Anna had seen the flash of the ring on her finger, an engagement ring. Something inside her froze, died, a stunned feeling of unreality overwhelmed her because she knew it could not be happening. She would have stayed there forever, except that Elaine called excitedly to her from the hall.

'He's here, Anna! Dan's home!'

He wasn't! He was simply visiting to let them see his fiancée, and jealousy tore into her, a feeling she had never had before.

When he saw her, he looked stunned. The long braid was gone now, her face fined out towards womanhood, her breasts softly tilted beneath the fine sweater she wore,

her legs long and slender beneath a swinging skirt. She was not the thin, ungainly oddity any more, and for a moment he just stood staring at her.

'Anna?' He looked as if he couldn't believe she had grown up. Then he came forward and looked down at her, and she made herself face him with a smile, forcing herself to be in some way natural; but she couldn't control her eyes and Dan stepped back, pointedly not touching her, shocked no doubt by the grief that was deep in her eyes.

'She's grown up!' Gavin had said proudly, and Dan's eyes narrowed, his face back to the usual good-humoured way he looked when he spoke to his father.

'She had to—one day. It was something that somehow never occurred to me!'

It was a week of torment, a never-ending nightmare because she couldn't dislike Daphne. There was something so sad, so vulnerable about her. Not that she had anything to be sad about. Dan was utterly attentive, and Anna pleaded that she had loads of work. College was looming ahead. More often than not she stayed in her room, making a pretence of working, meeting them at meal times and the long, interminable evenings when the family gathered in the drawing-room.

But she had little to say, and when Dan's eyes rested on her she felt as if she was choking. He had little to say to her too, and she supposed that he was annoyed that she ignored his fiancée. No doubt he thought her rude and grown into an even more prickly oddity. He looked at her as if he was angry, his face sombre and still, and there was definitely an atmosphere, although nobody else seemed to notice it.

When they went, she couldn't face it. She stayed in her room and looked through the lace curtains at them, her heart breaking as Dan said goodbye to everyone. When he looked for her, they all suddenly realised that she wasn't there, and Elaine started to move towards the house; but Dan stopped her and came in alone. He was coming to find her! He'd glanced up at her window and she'd drawn back fearfully. She couldn't face him! He had been angry all week, and if he saw her now he would be even more annoyed.

When he knocked on her door, she didn't answer. She moved to the farthest corner, almost cringing in her misery, her eyes on the door as if a fearful beast stood outside. When Dan opened the door, she drew further back to the wall, pressing herself against its hard surface.

He didn't speak. He just stood there looking at her, and then he closed the door and came inside, walking over to her, his hands cupping her face as she looked down.

His fingers speared into her long hair, his hands warm and strong, tilting her face to his, and they were just looking at each other, saying nothing.

'Would you let me go without a word? Aren't you coming to say goodbye?' he asked softly at last.

He was bringing her into the family goodbye, but she didn't feel like the family, she just felt lost and hopeless. The tears she had held inside filled her eyes and rolled on to her cheeks.

'Don't cry!' His fingers roughly wiped at her tears, but they fell faster still. This time she could not obey Dan and he pulled her into his arms, holding her tightly, tilting her face until she opened eyes that shone with

unhappy tears and looked at him. His eyes roamed over her face as if he was bewildered.

'Anna!' he whispered. 'Dear God! Where have you come from?'

She shook her head blindly, not understanding his words, everything weeping inside her. Where had she ever been but here, trying to please Dan?

His lips brushed hers and she responded wildly, out of all proportion to the gentle farewell. He looked stunned, unbelieving, and then he was kissing her, urgently and deeply, holding her close, his hands caressing her, moulding her to him as her arms wound around his neck and she gave herself up so wrongly to this onslaught of passion.

It was Gavin's voice that brought Dan back to his senses. He was calling from the hall, and Dan stiffened and moved back just a little, fastening the buttons of her blouse that had somehow parted, straightening his tie and looking at her with eyes that now held no expression at all.

'Take me with you!' She sobbed out the words without thought.

'In two weeks' time, I'll be married!' he said stonily, his eyes narrowing when she winced as if he had struck her. 'I only came back to let everyone see Daphne and to have a talk with my London publishers. In future, I'll live miles away.'

'You don't have to marry her!' she pleaded distractedly, ashamed even as she said it. 'How could you kiss me like that when you're going to be married?'

'You don't know a lot about men, Anna. Respond to any man like that and you'll get kissed like that.' His

face was cold, hard. 'I want to marry Daphne. Even if I didn't, she's pregnant!'

Every bit of colour drained from her face and he turned away.

'You're only seventeen,' he said harshly. 'You'll survive!'

He walked out as Gavin's voice got dangerously close. 'Did you find Anna?'

She heard the question and Dan's answer.

'Yes, I found her. I've said goodbye.'

He had. He had said goodbye in the most pitiless way possible, because now she knew that her feelings for Dan were not merely a child's possessive devotion. It would never heal, this wound he had inflicted, and she didn't move from the wall as they drove away out of her life.

It had healed, though. He had been perfectly right. For a while she had gone to pieces, but there was university, a new life and a secret feeling of shock inside her that Daphne was pregnant, even if Dan *was* going to marry her. Her idol toppled and fell, and she turned her thoughts to new things, new people. If Dan thought he could now order her about, he was mistaken! Perhaps tomorrow he would visit the solicitor and be told the news. She was glad she hadn't given him advance warning. *She* had had no advance warning!'

Fate caught up with her the very next day. When she woke up she had a terrible headache, and she staggered down to make herself a cup of tea long before anyone else was about. She took it back to her room, had two aspirin and got back into bed. She lay there on the edge of sleep for a long time before giving the whole idea up as hopeless.

It was ten o'clock when she got downstairs, and Dan was just walking into the house. She could tell by the look on his face that the game was up, and he looked at her sternly, indicating the study.

'In here, please!'

'I haven't had any breakfast yet,' she said quickly, fighting to keep any anxiety out of her voice. 'I woke up with a bad headache and went straight back to bed. I've got a headache now.'

'The weight of guilt, no doubt.' He took her arm and she had no choice but to go into the study, flinching as he shut the door loudly.

'Winters rang this morning to ask me to go to his office.' He looked at her coolly. 'You know Winters, I believe?'

'Er—he's the solicitor.' She was ducking away from those angry tawny eyes, and she knew it. He waited until she faced him, more desperate to get it over and done with than from any burst of courage, and his eyes were hard.

'Last night you had every opportunity to tell me about this gigantic role I'm supposed to play in your life!' he rasped. 'Instead you kept quiet, leaving me to find out from Winters. "You'll know of course from Anna that you're to be her guardian now that your father is gone?"' He was blazingly angry, and she had quite forgotten his ability to mimic almost any voice, usually with cruel insight. 'I had to be told all over again, of course, as you hadn't thought to enlighten me! Why did you keep quiet about it?'

He grasped her shoulders unexpectedly, and she was reminded once again how very strong Dan was.

'I thought you wouldn't want to be burdened with it.'

'Oh, I've no doubt whatsoever that you're the biggest burden possible!' he derided. 'Be that as it may, I've been designated your guardian and you knew all about it.'

'I'm twenty-one! The idea is ludicrous! I know full well that I don't inherit my father's money until I'm twenty-five, and I don't care at all. A guardian is something yet again! When my mother stipulated that, I was only a baby. She couldn't have meant it to go on for so long.'

'Maybe she had an insight into the sort of person you were going to grow up into!' he snapped.

Her face went white and he turned from her abruptly.

'Damn it all, Anna, why didn't you tell me?'

'Maybe I've got insight, too!' she said bitterly. 'Maybe I knew there would be this scene. There's trouble enough without this. What good is a guardian? I'm legally of age. I can do whatever I want to do, and I shall!'

'Who's going to stop you?' he murmured, turning back to her. 'Dad looked after you. You don't need looking after now, except perhaps...someone to watch over you.'

He sounded ruefully gentle, and she took courage from that.

'Tell him you won't do it, Dan,' she pleaded, looking up into the darkened eyes that watched her closely.

'I'm not sure what the legal complications of that would be. We can just say that I'm your guardian and then—forget all about it?' he suggested.

'You—you're willing to do that?'

She was wide-eyed with surprise, and he suddenly grinned down at her.

'Why not? I have enough to do without tucking you under my arm for the next four years. I don't even know you very well any more.'

'You never did!' It was out before she could stop it, and he stared at her hard, bringing a blush to her face.

'You think not? Perhaps I'll surprise you.'

She made for the door, counting the interview at an end, congratulating herself for getting away so lightly, but his voice stopped her.

'Come here!'

She could have been annoyed at the tone, but she was just surprised and walked back to him with only puzzlement on her face.

He took her arm and his other hand rested lightly against her forehead.

'I'm checking on the headache,' he said softly, amusement at the back of his eyes. 'I'm not at all sure what a guardian does, but that seems to be fairly basic.'

She wasn't particularly amused and she didn't like being close to him either. Still, if he was going to make guardian jokes, the idea might grow on him. She gave him a tight smile that contained no amusement whatever, but then it didn't need to—at that moment he seemed to have enough for both of them!

Keeping a smile on her face when Elaine's wedding day came around was a physical effort of Olympic proportions. During the two weeks before, Anna had endured each day by throwing herself heart and soul into wedding preparations. She was never still for a minute, and history seemed to be repeating itself as she skilfully avoided Dan, only having to face him at dinner and sometimes later in the evening when she could think of

no further excuse to keep out of the drawing-room. She just didn't feel comfortable with him. Four years had changed her. The slender thread that had always held her in his power had broken, and nothing had taken its place. He was like a stranger, and she had no idea whether this was because she felt differently and behaved differently, or whether it was all coming from Dan.

'You're exhausting yourself,' Edna said to her. 'There's no need for you to do absolutely everything. Miss Elaine is simply sitting dreamily around while you fly in all directions at once!'

'I'm loving it!' Anna said vigorously, but she wasn't loving it, she *needed* it! Dan had made no sign as to when he intended to leave. He seemed to have calls from his publishers or from America almost daily, and he spent a lot of time in the study, but he was always there, his presence all around her. At any time he might decide to interfere with her life, and she dreaded that. She didn't want to be entangled with Dan ever again.

The church was full when the day finally dawned, and Anna stood in the porch waiting for the bride to arrive, her time occupied completely by calming two very fidgety ten-year-old bridesmaids. There was the ceremony to come, then the reception at a large hotel in town, and then it would all be over. And the end of the vacation was drawing closer all the time. If she could just survive the few weeks! Elaine had not as yet realised the hidden animosity that was there between herself and Dan. If she found out, it would hurt her badly, and there had been enough hurts without breaking everything up completely. He was still a giant in Elaine's eyes, as he once had been in hers.

Elaine looked beautiful as she arrived with Dan's uncle, and Anna spent a few seconds arranging the bridal veil before the music started and they all went into church. She wouldn't look at Dan. She knew where he was, though. If it had been pitch-black, she would have been able to home in on him. What was he thinking now? Was he thinking about his own wedding day? Was he regretting that Daphne was not here, after all?

He was in the front pew, and as Elaine passed him he turned slowly, his eyes running with amusement over the two nieces of the groom and then lifting to look straight at Anna. She hadn't been expecting it, and for a moment their eyes held. Elaine had chosen the dresses with Anna's colouring in mind. The small bridesmaids wore white organza sprigged with tiny flowers so that they almost seemed to blend with the bridal veil that trailed behind. But Anna's dress was a rose-coloured silk, and with her olive-tinted skin and her jet-black hair she looked almost like a slender-stemmed rose herself.

It didn't help, though, to know she looked startlingly beautiful. When Dan looked at her, nothing helped at all. Something inside her resented him and she couldn't relax with him for even a minute. She tore her gaze away and stepped forward to take the bridal bouquet, forcing her mind to her duties, but she almost felt Dan's eyes boring into her as she stood opposite and the ceremony began.

When it was over and she walked down the aisle on the arm of the best man, she carefully avoided looking at anyone, her mind telling her steadily that it was almost over. There were the photographs around the church and then she could melt into the crowd.

As it was, she became the focus of all eyes. As they were getting ready for a shot of the wedding group she looked up and saw Bryan. He was all dressed for the wedding and he was standing a trifle anxiously at the church gate, trying to attract her attention.

'Bryan! Oh, please can you wait just a minute?' Anna called to the photographer, and then she was flying across the lawn, her hand on her head-dress, her face alight with joy and relief. Bryan to the rescue! Oh, bless him!

'You said you couldn't get away!' She launched herself at him and he caught her in a great hug, his pleasant face alight with laughter.

'I did a swap and a little fancy footwork. If I'd known this sort of greeting was on offer, I'd simply have walked out and told them to get on with it!'

He held her away and looked into her face, and she felt such a wave of affection that she reached up and kissed him right in front of everyone. He was so nice, so kind, not one bit of hardness in him. Why couldn't she just simply fall in love with him? Why hadn't she?

'Are you going to get me into one of the photographs?' He grinned down at her and she turned back to her duties as chief bridesmaid, but she still held tightly to his hand, as if it were a life-line, a protection from Dan and her uneasy feelings.

It all seemed to work. For a while Bryan was the focus of attention, and she forced herself to introduce him to Dan.

'This is Bryan Scott. Elaine told you about him,' she said with a warm smile at Bryan as they stood by Dan later. She was still clinging to Bryan's arm and he was beaming with pleasure. Normally he didn't get such at-

tention from her, although they went out with each other
regularly.

'The famous Dan Toren,' Bryan said with a disarming
grin. 'I've read every one of your books!'

Anna's heartbeats accelerated at that. She hoped he
wasn't going to say that he had borrowed them from
her! He didn't, and Dan didn't appear to be greatly
gratified by the compliment.

'It all helps with the sales,' he murmured laconically,
his eyes moving almost at once to Anna's glowing face.
She was making herself glow, congratulating herself on
her tremendous acting ability. 'I'm glad you're here,
though. It's the first time since I arrived home that Anna
has shown any sign of life. I was beginning to wonder
if she was ill. Obviously she was just pining!'

He gave her a rather sardonic look and then he was
gone; and Bryan glanced at her face, seeing the ani-
mation die out of it and a hidden anger take its place.

'Now, did I say something wrong?' he asked wryly.
'The praise didn't seem to go down too well.'

'I—it's not a good time for Dan,' she muttered,
looking away from Bryan's suddenly questioning eyes.
'He never got here in time for the funeral, and all this
so soon after... He did insist that things go on as
planned, but he must be feeling it.'

That was what it was, she told herself. Maybe Dan
thought she shouldn't have shown so much pleasure so
soon after Gavin's death. Perhaps this queer tightness
about him was grief that he couldn't show. An odd
feeling of protectiveness came over her and she turned
to speak to Dan, but he was already too far off. In any

case, he was as strained with her as she was with him; who could tell how he would react to sympathy? There was no getting close to Dan, and she didn't want to.

CHAPTER THREE

AT THE reception Anna continued to be animated, smiling and chattering to everyone, dragging Bryan around from one group to another until he complained. Elaine was grateful, but quite a few people looked at her oddly once or twice, and Dan seemed to be positively glowering.

She avoided him all the time, changing direction whenever he looked as if he was about to speak to her, but finally she went to freshen up, and when she came out of the powder-room Dan was waiting for her.

'Has anything happened?' He looked so grim that she felt sure that in her brief absence something of grave importance had occurred.

'Not yet,' he said severely. 'By some caprice of fortune you're still on your feet! I haven't seen you sit and relax for two weeks, and today just about crowns it. What's the matter with you?'

'Why, nothing. I'm really enjoying this!'

It was a shock that he wanted to care for her, and she forced herself back into a role that seemed to be quietly slipping away—but Dan was never fooled easily.

'The hell you are,' he bit out. 'You're glowing like an electric bulb that's just about to explode!'

'I can't just sit about when there's so much to do——' she began, but he took her arm in a firm grip.

'Nobody told me that you were expected to be the

bride's mother, the church warden and the caterer,' he rasped sardonically. 'I fondly imagined you were merely the chief bridesmaid!'

'I want Elaine to have a lovely day,' she protested, pulling to get away from his grasp. 'If I don't keep going...and then there's Bryan...'

'Spare me, Anna!' His face was suddenly harsh, his grip tightening almost to cruelty. 'Bryan is surrounded by a whole group of beauties, all fluttering their lashes at him. Don't worry though, his eyes have probably never left the door. He's not likely to look at anyone else when you're around, or even when you're not! Your act has nothing to do with him at all!'

He was bitterly mocking and annoyance flared across Anna's expressive face.

'I'd like to go back inside.' There was a great deal of tension in her voice, and his eyes lanced over her as his grip slackened to gentleness.

'You're so beautiful!' he said softly. His hand came slowly up to touch her face, his long fingers stroking her skin, and a shudder of feeling raced through her, scaring her.

'Please, Dan, I'm tired!'

He was making things difficult. She already had him classified. He had stopped being her idol four years ago. She couldn't feel the pain now, but she remembered it and her voice was bleak, brittle.

'I know,' he assured her aggressively, 'and I've no right to help. Isn't that what you're telling me so subtly? I'm supposed to be your guardian now, aren't I?' he added tightly. 'I ask myself why I should give up the job, even

though you are what romantic fiction calls a haughty beauty!'

They stared at each other angrily, then his face softened and his eyes began to smile.

'You're going to eat!' he said determinedly. 'I'm going to sit by you and see that you eat enough to keep you going. You can keel over when we get back home.'

He had her in a fix. It wasn't so easy to be angry with someone who smiled into your eyes, not when it was Dan, and she made a great effort to be natural, willing herself to relax as he led her back into the main room and guided her through it to the buffet.

'How long has the boyfriend got?' he asked idly as they ate.

'Only now, really. He'll have to go back tonight. He works hard, I hardly see him nowadays.' It was difficult to sound like a lovesick girl about Bryan, but she tried it. Instinct alone warned her that Dan must be kept firmly in his place, and his place was no longer close to her heart; all that had ended long ago. The smiling eyes were back to derision.

'It's going to be quite tricky when you go overseas or enter government,' he said mockingly. 'What will he do? Tag along behind?'

'He's not the tagging kind!' Anna said sharply.

'He looks devoted enough. Maybe he'll simply hitch his wagon to your star!'

'You make him sound like a wimp! He's not!'

'Everything about you swamps him,' Dan murmured in a taunting voice. 'You're too beautiful, too alive for any mere mortal, somehow. You don't look right together.'

Anna stood abruptly and put her plate down, the food only picked at.

'I'm full!' she asserted determinedly.

'And angry,' he added with a wry look at her flashing eyes. 'I'd rather have you angry than utterly self-controlled,' he said softly. 'It assures me that you're still alive, and as your guardian I need to know that.'

'You offered to forget the whole thing!'

'Except to watch over you,' he reminded her quietly.

She whirled around, her rose-coloured dress swinging, and walked off to find Bryan. What was Dan trying to do? She had given him no reason to suspect that she felt anything at all! She didn't! It was four years ago and it had only been a moment, a quick burst of passionate madness. Surely he remembered it like that, if he remembered it at all?

She went back to doing exactly what she had been doing before, wearing herself out, and a few minutes later Dan came back, leaning elegantly in the doorway, his eyes sardonic as she clung to Bryan and avoided him all over again.

It was terrible in the house without Elaine, but Anna was left well alone. She really did have some work to do for her finals and most of her time was now spent quite legitimately in her room. Also, she had a dreadful cold that wouldn't go. Dan had started another book and seemed quite content to work at Langford Hall in the study.

He hardly spoke to her at dinner times, and he apologised, saying that when he had a book running he hardly ever spoke. It suited her fine! The time was passing quickly. She worked all the time now, her mind only

half on her revision, the knowledge that he was there making it all that much harder.

She was walking in the woods after a hard morning of work when she met Dan, and it was clear he had come out to find her. It was awkward. They hardly spoke to each other now.

'You can't go on like this, Anna,' he insisted, falling into step beside her. 'Finals or not, this strain that you're forcing on yourself will break you up. You're going to be ill.'

'There's no reason to worry about me!' she managed through tight lips. She had thought of taking to her heels when she saw him, but it would have done little good. He was determined to talk to her, and she was well aware that he could have caught her.

'There's every reason to worry about you! That cold isn't clearing up. You hardly leave your room. You eat very little. This occasional walk is the only concession you make to health. You've always been brilliantly alive. You're fading almost before my eyes!'

'It's only for this week,' Anna assured him tautly, a brainwave suddenly striking her. 'Almost everyone will be going back now, gearing themselves up for the finals. I'm going back on Friday.'

'You don't look fit to go back yet!'

'I'm going, though. I'm quite used to making my own decisions. In any case, it will give me time to be with Bryan before the exams swallow me up!'

He was silent, suddenly tense and brooding.

'Are you really going to marry him?' he asked unexpectedly. 'Is Elaine right when she hears wedding bells?'

'At the moment we're both too busy. Eventually, I suppose,' Anna said in a stiff voice. The thought of marriage made her tighten up inside. The finality of it. It was final for Dan! She had never asked him if he was going to marry. He had told her in no uncertain terms about his plans four years ago!

'Do you live with him?'

The question took her breath away and she had to swallow hard before she answered. 'I live in hall!' It came out angrily, and her face was flushed and embarrassed, but he never even seemed to notice.

'I'm aware of that. That's not what I meant and you know it!' There was a raw sound to his voice that astonished her. She supposed that he was protecting his new-found ward, trying it out for size. It filled her with fury. She didn't need Dan poking into her life. He seemed reasonably content not to have his wife with him! He could get on with his writing!

'You mean do I sleep with him? It's none of your damned business!' She whirled round and glared at him. 'I don't ask you personal questions. What Bryan and I do is our affair. We love each other,' she added in a choking voice.

They didn't. They were fond of each other. She supposed that he could loosely be called a boyfriend, whatever that really meant, but they were both too occupied with the world of learning to be too much together. It was just a comfortable arrangement. They went out with each other, had done so for two years, they went about together, usually with other people too. She would never let Dan find that out. There was no way he was going to imagine that she still clung to the memory of four years ago.

'Love each other? Do you?' He grasped her shoulders and swung her back to face him when she was just about to march off. 'He doesn't look capable of controlling you!'

No. She realised that Dan thought Bryan a mere boy. It had been written all over his face at the wedding.

'Yes, we love each other,' she said heatedly, 'and that being the case, I don't need controlling.'

'You always did, apparently,' he said quietly, 'and yet, never when I was there.'

'I was scared of you,' Anna murmured in a strained voice. 'I thought of you as a—a rather alarming big brother.'

'All the time?' he asked derisively, his hands tightening.

'I grew up and realised that you weren't a giant!' The long fingers were probing the delicate bones around her neck, and she felt almost unable to breathe. 'I don't really know you now at all. People grow apart.'

'Yes. Nothing stays the same. Lives change, and not always for the better. I went away to make a fortune and succeeded. In doing so, I lost a whole life.'

He dropped his hands and turned to the path, and she felt again the great rush of protectiveness. He had lost his father. She knew what it had done to her; it was even worse for Dan. She was suddenly torn apart with remorse, and her hand went out to touch his arm.

'Oh, Dan!'

He looked at her for a long moment and then smiled, his hand covering her fingers.

'Oh, what the hell!' he said briskly. 'There's no future in wishing.'

He put his arm around her shoulders and turned her to the path, walking with her back to the house, never noticing the look on her face. Frighteningly, she had been back in the past for a second. She wasn't going back there! She didn't feel the same now.

'When are you going back to the Bahamas and your little island?' she asked after a minute, wanting to make some ground for normal conversation and wanting rather desperately to get Dan as far away as possible.

'When things have settled down,' he answered quietly. 'I can work at Langford Hall quite easily. I only need a typewriter and it never leaves my side. I want everything settled, and Elaine back from her honeymoon. I'll stay until you've done your finals.'

'No! There's no need. You mustn't come down to Oxford to see me!'

There was an unnatural urgency in her voice and he stiffened, his arm dropping away from her.

'I have no such intention,' he said coolly. 'I realise that you'll be busy and that every spare minute is Bryan's. I'll be quite content to be at the other end of a telephone in case you need—in case *either* of you needs me.'

'I would have thought that your wife needed you,' she said tartly. 'The longer you stay here, the longer you're going to be apart. We have, after all, managed without you for four years, and three years before that!'

'I'm aware of my shortcomings!' he grated. 'If I'd been here over the last four years I would have seen more of Dad. I confess to neglect. I am not, however, neglecting my wife. I don't have one!'

His tone warned her to say no more, but she stopped, almost open-mouthed, and he stopped too, turning to look at her coldly.

'You—you said you were going to marry Daphne!' she said in a stunned voice, her mind racing to contain this. 'She had a great big ring and...'

'In the end, we didn't fancy it,' he informed her impatiently.

He just stood there, his hands in his pockets, his tawny eyes sardonic, and her colour mounted as she understood why he was so scathing. Daphne had been pregnant and yet... She could never have imagined that Dan would let anyone down. Did he know when he was here four years ago that he was not going to marry that poor woman? How many more were there? Was this what living in the world of best sellers and films did to a person, or had she been too young before to notice what Dan was really like?

He must think her very young and foolish that she still had illusions of love. Or maybe he thought her head was too filled with academic thoughts, ambitious desires to be in banking or government.

'Then, as you're footloose and fancy free, you can do as you like, can't you?' she managed coldly. 'It will be nice to know that there's someone at the hall besides Edna.'

'Why should you care?' he jeered. 'As I understand, you're not coming back!'

'There's nothing to come back to,' Anna countered. 'People make a home, not a collection of old stones.'

'I've been called many things, but never an old stone,' he said ironically. 'Not that I'm surprised. I suppose the island is my home now, if I have one. When Elaine left,

the last warmth went from Langford Hall. Why are we bothering to keep it, Anna? I'm not welcome, and you don't want to be!'

He turned back towards the house as the words tore into her heart. Dan—unwelcome? She had loved him. He had toppled from his position as idol, and his latest revelation had confirmed that he was not what she had imagined, but there were memories, all of Dan.

'Dan!' Her voice was soft and he glanced round at her, seeing everything on her face.

'Sympathy?' he taunted. 'I don't really need that. I don't need a collection of old stones, either!'

'Then sell it,' she said bitterly, his mockery stifling any further gentleness.

'Oh, no,' he said softly. 'It's had a Toren there for generations, and one day there'll be another. I haven't married so far, but I will. Besides, you begged me not to sell only two weeks ago. If your heart changes so rapidly, it's likely to change back again. As Elaine is married there's only you and I. We'll leave it until you know your own mind and then discuss it.'

'When I marry, I'll also have a house,' Anna said tightly.

'Let me know when the time comes,' Dan said smoothly. 'Of course, a doctor couldn't afford it, but you'll have your inheritance. And if you're in government, who knows? I might sell it to you!'

He wanted to drive her back to Oxford, but she refused. She had her own car, in any case, and she didn't think she could face a drive so far with a totally silent Dan beside her. He shrugged and left her to her own affairs, and she went off feeling bleak, miserable and somehow

guilty. The drive seemed to be never-ending, and on the way she acquired a cough, her cold going one miserable stage further.

It was good to be back with ordinary people, although at the moment there was little about them that was ordinary. They were strained, and showed it in very different ways. In her own little group of friends there were a few very outgoing people, and she joined them during the evenings of the last week before the finals in a little revelry, very minor, nothing more than a few pizzas and a glass of wine at the very noisy wine-bar in town, a well-known haunt of students in term-time. She absolutely willed her cold away, but it stayed there and refused to go, getting tighter by the day. Nobody noticed much. They were too busy making merry and worrying.

On the last weekend she decided that the Friday night was her very last time out. If she had been sensible she would have spent these evenings in bed, but she didn't feel like being sensible. Her time with Dan had shaken her more than she was willing to admit, and every moment spent alone was a moment that allowed him to steal into her thoughts. She couldn't afford to allow him to be there ever again.

Things were noisier than usual on Friday night, as nerves soared to a crescendo, and although Anna didn't feel much like making merry she tried. The noise rang through her head, the smoke made her eyes run and she began to feel that she would need help to get back to her room. It was useless to call Bryan. He was on duty as usual, and he would only give her a lecture on the subject of a neglected cold.

She never saw Dan until he was right in front of her, towering over her grimly, and she gaped at him stupidly,

giving the decided impression that she had been joining in much too heartily with the merry-making. She didn't quite believe that it was Dan. He had to be a mirage, but when she closed her eyes and opened them again he was still there, looking angrier than ever.

'Come along!'

He reached for her and took her arm, pulling her to her feet, and several forms of hazy protest rang out that darkened his already furious face.

'Hey, Anna! Who's the Superman?'

'Unhand her, sir!'

Everyone collapsed into laughter and there was no attempt to stop him. It was all light-hearted, and she realised that if she was being abducted there was nobody in a fit state to assist. She *was* being abducted! Dan propelled her to the door and out into the open air, where she began to cough almost uncontrollably.

His sympathy was entirely absent. He waited with mounting impatience and then marched her off along the street to his car, the one he had brought with him when he'd first arrived at Langford Hall.

'What are you doing? Why are you here? I don't want to...'

'Get in!'

The words were not really needed. He bundled her into the car and it seemed that only seconds later they were pulling into the car park of one of the very best hotels.

Getting out was not difficult either; he hauled her out unceremoniously and her feet hardly touched the ground as she was taken through the rather forbidding doors past an equally forbidding doorman into an opulent foyer. Dan was more forbidding than anything or

anyone, and she still hadn't recovered from the shock of his sudden arrival.

Recovery came when she found herself in his room and heard him ordering black coffee for one immediately.

'What are you doing?' she demanded, standing on decidedly shaky legs and looking at him furiously.

His looks were the more furious.

'I'll speak to you when you've got some coffee inside you and when you can see straight!'

It all dawned on her with astonishing speed.

'You think I'm drunk!'

'I know it!' he bit out.

'And for once in your life, you're *wrong*! I've had one lemonade with ice and nothing more! And you can change that coffee order if it's for me. I don't like black coffee!'

He looked at her very hard, and then lifted the phone and changed the order to a tray of tea. Anna sat down, her legs finally giving out.

'What the hell were you doing with all that rowdy lot?' he grated, coming to tower over her again.

'That rowdy lot were students letting off steam before the dreaded finals! You were a student once—I suppose you never did anything like that?'

'Was Bryan there?' he enquired with great suspicion still on his face, her remarks ignored.

'He was not! He's working, as usual. What are you doing here, Dan? If you think I'm going to put up with this guardian nonsense, then . . .'

'I came to say goodbye. I'm going back to the Bahamas, back to the island.'

He turned away and her face fell, a wave of something that might well have been dismay racing over her.

'Oh!'

'Oh?' He turned back and looked at her, narrow-eyed. 'I did wonder for a moment if you'd had prior warning of my departure and were celebrating the fact!'

'I told you what we were doing,' she muttered vaguely. Her head came up and she looked at him with tired, dark eyes. 'I thought you were staying until my finals were over?'

'For what reason?' he asked coolly. 'You don't need a guardian. We're not friends, not relatives, so what the hell are we? The moment we meet we begin a battle. There's no reason for me to stay.'

'I suppose not.' She looked away, and after a moment he came and tilted her face.

'Have you eaten?'

'No—no. I—I didn't much fancy a gooey pizza and...'

He wasn't listening. He was at the phone, ordering sandwiches with the tea.

'You'll not be popular. The tea will be already on the way.'

'Just so long as they don't make the mistake of expressing displeasure, they'll be all right,' he assured her grimly, and she didn't think they would express displeasure when they saw Dan's face like that, tight and angrily frustrated.

'How did you find me?' She was watching him in an almost drugged fashion, and he glanced at her irritably.

'I asked where the students gathered, then I followed the noise.'

'Why did you bother? You could have sent me a card from the Bahamas!'

His irritation hurt, and the fact that it did made her speak coldly, through tight lips.

'I thought you'd want to be good and sure that I'd left. You can actually come and see me on to the plane if you want; that way you'll be certain that you're free!'

Free? He meant alone. She looked away and he was suddenly silent, but it was a silence she could actually hear. It didn't matter. She pleased him no more now than she had done all her life, and she didn't care. She didn't even care if he remembered the way she had reacted to him when he had said goodbye to her four years ago. He probably remembered it with disgust. What did it matter? She was so tired.

She slipped her jacket off and curled up in a chair, tiredness washing over her, and she was almost asleep when a waiter came and placed a tray discreetly by her on the low table.

'Eat, drink and be merry!' Dan said caustically, pouring tea for her and indicating the sandwiches. She didn't want them, but somehow she thought she should eat them. It was a good idea to duck when Dan was furious, and she had never seen him in a worse mood.

She fell asleep. Dan wasn't talking. He was pacing about the room and then he disappeared out of the door. The next thing she knew, he was shaking her gently.

'Come along! Bedtime.'

'Are you taking me back now?' It was all she could do to keep her eyes open, and she staggered as he let her go.

'No. You've got a room next to mine and you're staying here tonight, right under my intent scrutiny.'

'I can't.'

'You've never stayed out all night before?' he asked scathingly, and as he had clearly made his mind up about that she didn't disillusion him. He looked very grim

indeed as he led her to the next room and pointed to a soft-looking bed that beckoned to her invitingly.

The cough came back with worse effect and he just walked out, not caring if she choked. What could she expect? He had never cared! Yes, he had, she argued to herself. He had never doted on her, but he had always been kind. She was the one who had been awkward when she really analysed it. Her lifetime's obsession with him had made her shy and prickly, impossible to deal with. He was just fed up with her now, and small wonder.

She suddenly realised that she had nothing with her, not even a nightie, but she was not leaving the bed now, it looked too good. She struggled to undress, sitting down to take off her shoes and then resting for a minute, the cough exhausting her.

Dan walked in while she was like that, and she was too far gone to care that she was only in her slip.

'I've been down to get this,' he said quietly, holding up a bottle of some cough mixture. 'You're quite sure that you haven't been drinking? These things are sometimes dangerous after drink. They make you drowsy.'

'One lemonade,' Anna said wearily. 'Nothing could make me more drowsy than I am now!'

He gave her some on a spoon and she sat like a rag doll as he carefully screwed the bottle-top on and put the spoon down. Her eyes were closed and she couldn't make the effort to open them.

'Into bed,' he said softly, and he lifted her up and placed her on the cool sheets, covering her carefully and flicking off the lights.

'Thank you, Dan,' she murmured, but he said nothing and she was asleep before he left the room.

In the morning she was awakened by a maid bringing breakfast to her, and she sat up in bed and managed to eat most of it, knowing that Dan would come to check up on her. He did, just as she was finishing, and this morning she was not so tired as to be unaware that her slip was her only covering.

'You can get up now!' he informed her stiffly as she hastily pulled the sheets to her neck. 'I shall be checking out almost at once. I'll take you back to college and then I'll be on my way.'

It made her feel incredibly lonely, and she couldn't think of a thing to say to him. All she could do was sit there and stare.

'When you go to college, you should report to your tutor and tell her that you're ill.' He was staring back at her aggressively, and her eyes fell before the punishing look.

'I've only got a cold.'

'And utter exhaustion! Of such small beginnings, pneumonia is made. By the look of your companions last night, I would imagine they would ask rather vaguely where you were and then forget all about it.'

'We're all adults! We take care of ourselves. I don't suppose anyone took care of you when you were at university.'

'I had a bit more muscle about me than you have, and I hadn't just organised a wedding, lost my father, worked myself to a standstill and caught a cold. I tend to do one thing at a time!'

'It's just unfortunate that it's the finals,' she muttered, uneasy about his intense looks and his aggressive voice.

'True! No doubt you'll be taking them again next year,' he murmured sarcastically.

That put the cat among the pigeons! She felt a wave of fury, and without thinking she threw back the bedding and swung her legs out of bed, standing to glare at him.

'You're not likely to know! By then I'll be really on my own, thank goodness. If you imagine you can cart me away from my friends, dump me in a hotel and then come to lecture me the next day like a bearded old uncle, then you can think again! We know exactly where we stand on the subject of who wants a guardian. The island is calling—go!'

A little of the steam faded as she realised he was watching her through amused, narrowed eyes, the tawny gaze skimming over her small, vibrantly angry figure.

'Very well,' he agreed, 'I'll go back to where I belong, but don't utterly discount my advice. Lose any more weight and you'll be more skinny than interesting!'

Frighteningly, the memory of his hands caressing her four years ago filled her mind. She could almost feel them sensuously stroking her skin. Colour flooded into her cheeks and his lips twisted wryly before he walked out of the room, closing the door with a snap.

During the time of her finals, she realised just what Dan had seen when he had accused her of making herself ill. The great strain of Gavin's death, the effort needed to be at all natural with Dan in the house, the work she had put in for Elaine's wedding and her work for her exams had left her on the edge of exhaustion. The cold had taken weeks to even begin to go, dragging her down even further, and she knew she should have seen a doctor.

She looked at herself in the mirror and saw exactly what Dan had seen, only now, almost at the end of her exams, she looked even worse. Her hair was back in a braid because she had no time to bother with it. She wasn't eating and never went out. The rose flush of her cheeks had gone, the olive-tinted skin was lifeless and pale. She had lost so much weight that her thick, heavy hair seemed too much for her head. Nobody seemed to have noticed, and she was glad about that. When the hustle of the exams was over, they were going to notice then. Right now everyone was completely self-absorbed.

Only her brain seemed to work, and she fought her way through the finals as if it was a battle with no end in sight. In truth she had been devastated by being near to Dan again. He had always meant too much to her, and she couldn't face the fact that now he had betrayed someone. When she was alone she found her mind searching for him, for the old Dan, the Dan she had loved so fiercely. It did nothing to help her in her state of exhaustion. It made matters worse, and sleep was always just out of her reach. He was gone, far, far away. She had images of him before her mind as she lay life-lessly waiting for morning, the sound of some distant sea murmuring in her ears.

The finals finished but she was unable to relax, not quite believing that it was all over. The others were cel-ebrating but she had nothing to celebrate. All the years of work seemed to have been wasted. She might as well have never taken the exams at all. Bryan phoned her regularly but she didn't want to see him; everything was too much effort, even going for a meal was exhausting, and she kept the fact from Bryan. She needed no lec-tures. That was Dan's sphere.

She decided to stay on, to try to get some rest. She really had no idea what to do, in any case. At home she had talked blithely of going directly overseas. She had spoken of an interim job doing just anything until the exam results were out, an idea that had received Dan's frowning disapproval. She was in no fit state to do anything at all, and she had already turned down two interviews for jobs because she couldn't face getting ready to attend any interview.

In fact, she had nowhere to go at all. Certainly she could go not back to Langford Hall. It would be terrible without Elaine, and she would be thinking of Dan every day. She wasn't even sure if she had the right to go back now. Whatever he had originally said, they had become almost enemies before he went away. He had not communicated at all. At least it was quiet here now. She was too pent up to sleep at nights, but she slept in short naps during the day. At least the cold had gone. Maybe next week she would feel fit enough to get out of here and begin a new life...

CHAPTER FOUR

SHE was asleep when Dan came, lying on top of the bed, sleeping as she sometimes did now in short bursts of time when exhaustion refused to let her mind continue functioning. She opened her eyes and he was in her room, standing over her, his face furious. Her tutor was hovering nervously in the background, not at all her usual forbidding self, and although Anna spoke Dan ignored her and turned his considerable wrath on the hapless woman in the doorway.

'Why wasn't I called before this? Is it the policy of this college to allow a student to simply fade away without informing relatives?'

He was violently angry and Anna couldn't get a word in anywhere. She couldn't believe that he was here!

'The activity—the finals—so many students... They are, after all, grown up, Mr Toren! Many students can't take the strain of finals. It was only when she stayed on and never left her room that we realised...'

'She's leaving her room now!' Dan grated. 'If there are any formalities, then you'd better complete them. In just about fifteen minutes I'll have her out of here!'

The swift bang of the door showed that tutors were rarely spoken to like this, and Anna was now sitting up on the bed, feeling shaky and slightly disorientated.

'Dan! What are you doing here? I don't understand.'

'They sent for me,' he said testily. 'At least, they rang the Hall and I was there. One more day and there would

have been nobody there at all because I'd decided to go back to the island, after all. By sheer chance I was at the house. They had no idea that the family is now split asunder, and apparently they could get no sense out of you!'

'I—I don't remember them asking,' she said shakily.

'No.' His eyes narrowed on her pale face. 'I don't have to be a doctor to recognise mental and physical exhaustion. You probably don't know what day it is. Where was the boyfriend while you were fading away?'

'I've not been out. Bryan is working all hours and I...'

'Well, you're coming out now. Right out!' Dan rasped angrily.

'I can stay here. I...'

'It may have escaped your attention, Anna, but there isn't a finals student in the place! They've finished and gone! Were you going to stay here until you were found by an inquisitive porter? You're coming home with me.'

'I'm not going back to Langford Hall! I thought... Why aren't you in the Bahamas?'

'I decided to wait a while. In any case, you're not going back to Langford Hall. I said you were coming home with me, and that's the island. I've already got my ticket and I'll have yours within the hour. They'll certainly not charge full fare for you!' he added sarcastically. 'You're nothing more than a set of beautiful bones!'

'I can't go to the island!' she gasped, her hand anxiously at her collar, plucking agitatedly at the white cotton. 'I can't go there because...'

Daphne would have been there! Maybe that was where... She couldn't face that!

'You're coming with me, Anna!' He suddenly knelt down beside her, looking up into her pale, distressed face. 'I won't leave you,' he said, softly but determinedly. 'You're on the point of total collapse. I'm keeping you with me until I can be quite sure that you're safely restored to your rightful mind.'

'There's nothing wrong with my mind!' Anna assured him with a burst of annoyance. 'I'll go to Elaine and Steve.'

'They're newly-weds! Have a heart,' he said mockingly. 'In any case,' he finished, standing and casting a grim eye around the room, 'I'm going back to the island and you're going to be right there beside me when I fly out. It's no use arguing! Any argument will only make you more strained, and I can simply pick you up and bundle you into a trunk, by the look of you. Better to travel first class!'

'I won't have a guardian!' She didn't feel much like fighting him, but she made a token protest. In actual fact, she couldn't stop looking at him. He had appeared like a fury, but she felt safe, her desire to cling to him only her physical weakness.

'You've got one, baby,' he grated harshly, 'and after these few weeks I'm beginning to have a great deal of admiration for your mother's foresight. Left to yourself, you'd never survive!' He simply threw her wardrobe doors open and began to pack for her; and when she protested and stood up, he ordered her sharply back to the bed. In this tornado mood it seemed to be best to obey, and she watched him with wide eyes as he strode about, packing her things methodically.

'By the look of you nothing here fits you any more in any case,' he speculated grimly. 'Anything else you need we'll get in Nassau.'

'You—you can't just spirit me away like this, Dan!' she began plaintively, wondering why she couldn't fight him but knowing that she couldn't. He came and took her arm, leading her to the mirror.

There were dark smudges beneath eyes that seemed to fill her thin face; even her blouse looked too big for her. She seemed to be all hair and eyes, like a mere ghost of herself. Where had the days gone since the finals? She just couldn't remember.

'I intend to spirit you away,' he assured her grimly. 'I really pity anyone who tries to stop me!'

Before the hour was up she was in Dan's car, heading towards London, too exhausted to protest any more, her eyes constantly returning to his tight profile and the strong, graceful hands on the wheel.

'If you hired this car, it must be costing a fortune,' she said after a while. 'You've had it for ages.'

This inconsequential little remark merely drew his eyes to her in a quick flash of surprise. Maybe he thought she had gone mad.

'I bought it when I arrived, as a matter of fact!' He dismissed the subject as being trifling, but she hung on to it grimly, the whole thing taking on a great puzzle in her tired mind.

'What will we do about selling it? Will we have to sell it when we get to London?'

Suddenly she sounded like a child again. It had always been 'we'. What will we do about this, Dan? What will we say to them, Dan? He glanced at her worriedly, his eyes on her hands clasped tightly in her lap. For a

moment he had almost expected to see the thin little hands clenched together, the way they had always been when he had spoken to her, but they were a woman's hands, pale and slender, the bones of her wrists too pronounced.

'At the moment I don't care if we abandon it on the M4!' he said grimly. His hand came and closed over hers. 'It's quite a way yet. Go to sleep, Anna.'

'All right. I'm really tired, Dan.'

'Yes.' His voice was strange, husky, and she puzzled about that for almost a whole minute before she closed her eyes and slept, her head falling against his shoulder, her eyes not seeing the bleak look about his face as he drove on towards the airport.

After that it was all dreamlike. They stayed overnight in an hotel and, though she tried to sleep at once, Dan called a doctor who looked at her as if she had done it all deliberately and said she was suffering from exhaustion and the aftermath of a severe cold. She could fly, he said, but she must rest for some time afterwards. Dan received this news with raised eyebrows and a disgusted look, muttering as he closed the door on the departing doctor that he could have diagnosed all that himself.

Anna slept deeply for the first time in ages, her taut muscles relaxing. She ate a light supper merely to please Dan, her eyes following him as he went silently from the room and switched out her light. She was worried about everything, about the island, about being where Dan had taken others. She was back to her childish jealousy, only part of her mind anchored safely. She had loved him so much. How would she be when they got to the island? What about Dan's son? Did Dan see them still? Did he acknowledge the child? For four years she had imagined

him married. Four years of her life had been built on that fact. Perhaps Daphne would visit? She drifted away into sleep, her hand clutching the sheets, and the sleep was black and deep, healing.

The islands lay like jewels in a clear, green sea, frothy white breakers edging them, and Anna gazed down, entranced. From the air the scene was everyone's dream of paradise: coral, ocean and sky. For the moment she was content, more content than she had been since Dan had gone away and left her. It was a brief interval of time, she knew, but for now there was no use denying it.

'Can we see your island from here?'

She turned to him eagerly, and for the first time he smiled. He had looked after her almost ferociously, but he was tense and sombre, clearly not wishing to have her here at all, no more patient with the thought of guardianship than she was. It was a relief therefore to see the old smile edge his lips and soften his tawny eyes.

'No. It's too small. It's just over the rim of the horizon. If we were higher, perhaps. It's a very small island, only three square miles. Many of the islands are like that, some smaller.'

'Does it have a name?'

'Yes. Amara Cay.' He pronounced the word 'key'.

'What does that mean?' Her interest seemed to pull him even further from the sombre mood that had been on him since he had rescued her from college, and he leaned back and relaxed more.

'Cay, means "small island". There are over seven hundred in the Bahamas, maybe more. Nobody is exactly certain.'

'What does Amara mean? It's a beautiful name.'

'Amara? I don't know. Perhaps it was the name of some pirate's mistress. These islands were once haunted by buccaneers and very dangerous. There's quite a lot of smuggling going on even these days. It's not a very good idea to sail close inshore at night. You might say that pirates still haunt the place.'

'But not the sort with gold ear-rings and cutlasses!' Anna retorted wryly. He was gently teasing, just as he could be at times, the Dan she had adored all her life; a great wave of happiness washed over her. It was impossible to continue being suspicious and cool when he was so good to her. She sighed deeply, a smile on her still pale face.

'Are you going to enlighten me about that blissful sigh?' he enquired quietly.

'It's sheer contentment!' she exclaimed, completely unguarded for the moment. 'I was thinking that...'

With a small shock she realised how unguarded she was. She had been about to blurt out her thoughts, tell him that she was happy for this little while. Perhaps when they reached Amara Cay there would be another woman there. Perhaps he lived with someone, as he had so readily asked if she lived with Bryan.

'Yes?'

'I wonder what they're all doing at home?' she murmured evasively, and Dan's smile became wry.

'The sigh was a feeling of contentment that whatever they're doing, you aren't?' he asked drily.

'I never told Bryan that I was leaving!' she said suddenly, the idea striking her guiltily. 'He'll be frantic.'

'You can send a message when we land,' Dan assured her. 'As he was too busy to notice your slide into illness,

he'll probably not even have discovered that you've gone.'

'You don't understand about Bryan and I!' Anna protested, realising that she must keep up this pretence of a love-affair. After all, nothing had changed.

She was simply daydreaming. The strain of the last few months had left her vulnerable, and she didn't want to fight Dan any more.

His life didn't contain any room for her. Right now he was simply looking after her, feeling it to be a duty. It meant nothing more than that. He was treating her like a sister. If it had been Elaine, he would have done the same thing.

'Understand? No, I don't!' he said, with a sort of quiet savagery that made her cringe.

It was the end of their small time of contentment, and Anna stared down at the vision of enchantment on a turquoise sea, but now the happiness had gone, reality had taken its place. He had brought her here to get better. Whatever time there was would be brief. It had to be. She and Dan had nothing in common.

Nassau was noisy and crowded and hot. The climate was in fact perfect, but after England and in her present state of health it was not long before Anna felt very jaded.

'We'll get straight out to the island!' Dan said, after one all-encompassing look at her that took in her pale face and tired eyes.

'I think I'll have to have my hair cut short,' she murmured, lifting it away from her neck fretfully.

'Not at this moment,' he assured her. 'Give things a few days and you'll get quite used to any heat. You can braid it as you used to do.'

'It's too heavy!' she complained stubbornly.

'It's quite beautiful! If you have it cut off, you'll be sorry later, and it will be too late then. Drastic actions have a way of backfiring, and there's no going back.'

His tone surprised her and she turned to look at him, but he was busy looking for a taxi and not paying any attention to her at all, his face back to the tension he had shown all the time.

They were dropped at a quayside and the heat was not so bad there, with a breeze blowing off the sea. It was fascinating, too. Behind the quay was an outdoor market, and boats were coming in even then from the islands with fruit, vegetables, conches, crabs and lobsters. It was so colourful that Anna could have watched all day.

They knew Dan too, calling out to him, laughing and joking, their dark faces beaming at Dan and turning enquiringly to Anna. Dan didn't enlighten anyone, and she felt guilty. They were probably used to seeing him here with Daphne, because why they were here soon became apparent.

'Here we go!' Dan motioned her forward, the taxi driver carrying some of their bags, and they were soon stepping into a smart white launch moored at the quayside.

Dan paid off the taxi driver and then settled Anna in the cabin below deck, sliding back the window and letting in the fresh breeze.

'Sit here for a minute and recover. I'll not be long.'

She watched anxiously, but he was just going to the market, and soon he was back with armfuls of fruit and vegetables, many of which she had never seen before, a laughing, dark-skinned trader walking beside him, carrying more.

This was how Dan lived, in this warm, exciting place. No wonder he never came back. There was everything he needed here and there was nobody to question how he lived or who he lived with. A gloom settled on Anna and she closed her eyes to try and shut out the vista of the future. It would not be shut out. Dan was slipping back into her heart and she was too weary to fight him away.

'Anna?' He was in the cabin and she hadn't even known. His hands were tight on her upper arms as he crouched down and looked into her face. 'Are you feeling ill?'

'No. No, I'm fine!' She smiled wanly, but he still looked worried.

'Come up on deck and we'll get under way. The breeze will do you good. When we get home, Josie will put you straight to bed!'

'I don't want to go to bed!' she protested as she followed him out on to the gleaming deck and stood beside him as he cast off and started the powerful, growling engines.

'It's "do as you're told" time!' he said lightly, but she could tell from his face that he was worried. She felt even more guilty. She didn't even ask who Josie was. Time to mind her own business and hold her tongue. She would be exactly what Dan wanted her to be, and then she would go home and forget all about him. The thought that she now had no home came rushing into her mind, but she pushed it firmly out. She would not be a burden to Dan or anyone else!

Once out in the open sea the launch leapt forward like a greyhound, and Anna felt a wave of exhilaration as she clutched the rail and stood beside Dan. He was en-

joying it, a sort of wild, free look on his face, and she knew exactly how he felt.

They simply flew over the radiant waters, past the sandy beaches of other islands, some palm-fringed almost to the shoreline, others bright with blossoming trees. It was a wonderland, a place of dreams, and Anna gripped the rail tightly, her black hair blowing behind her. She could almost feel health returning.

'Enjoying it?' Dan cast her a flashing sideways look, and a shock of feeling hit her deep inside, in no way controllable. It stunned her and she turned away rapidly.

'Oh, yes!'

She said nothing more, but when she glanced at him secretly there was a small smile back on his lips and her gloomy heart lifted again. For now, she was here with Dan and, even if it was only for this wild ride over the shimmering sea, it was worth every moment of misery that had gone. It was useless to deny it, there had always been a magic about being with Dan. At home, in Langford Hall, the memories had been too mixed up, the misery of his going still real after four years, but now they were beginning to fade. Everything was new and Dan was golden, looking after her, right beside her.

'Look!' He pointed down below the waves as he slackened off speed and the boat began to cruise in more shallow waters.

She looked down over the side and gasped. It was like a fairyland, a world of coral and tiny fish. It was so clear that she could see the white sandy bottom, the coral white and faintly pink, shaped like castles and caverns, where the fish played and darted.

'It's beautiful!'

'I'll take you scuba diving,' he promised. 'As soon as you're a little stronger.'

'Aren't there sharks?' she asked fearfully, her eyes still glued to the fascinating underwater scene.

'Not inside the reef. There's a lovely bay at the other side of the island. I dive there.'

She was so mesmerised, so enchanted, that she had never noticed that the boat was slowing even more, and when she looked up they were nosing in towards a sandy beach, palms and flowering bushes skirting the water edge, white rocks standing above the beach, and set back behind a small landing-stage a low white house surrounded by bright gardens. Dan's island, Amara Cay!

She stared at it with wide eyes, her hand holding back her blowing black hair, and Dan edged the boat to the landing-stage and cut the motors, leaping out to tie up and then reaching forward to take her hand. She was still staring around dazedly as he spanned her narrow waist and lifted her from the deck and out on to the steady footing of the small quay.

'I can hardly believe it!' she breathed. 'I often wondered what your island was like. I—I'm actually here!'

'At last!' he finished in an odd voice, and when she looked up he was watching her intently, the tawny eyes moving over her face with a look she could not at all understand.

'What do you think of Amara Cay?' he asked softly, but he was thinking of something else, she could tell that.

'It looks as if it might be heaven,' she said with a trembling little laugh.

'Pretty close to it, sometimes,' he said quietly.

He looked away and turned her to the house, and she knew he was glad to be back, glad to be away from England, Langford Hall and the depressing times. After all, he never came back now, he only wanted to be here. He had told Elaine that as soon as he had finished any work at the studios he was back to his island like a shot. If it had not been for his father's death and Elaine's wedding, she would never have seen him again, in all probability.

The thought sobered her and she bit her lip, suddenly feeling shaky and altogether let down after the exhilaration of the ride here. All at once the house seemed far away, the walk to it too much. She was unexpectedly swept off her feet, and she gave a startled gasp as Dan swung her up into his arms.

'You're flagging, madam!' he insisted when she begged to be allowed to walk. 'A few more yards and you'll be a lot closer to Josie and bed!'

He was laughing again, the queer mood gone, and she put her arm around his neck to steady herself.

'Who is Josie? And what will she think if we arrive like this?' she protested.

'Josie runs the house for me, her husband Abe does the garden and everything else, and she'll take one look at you and assume that I've caught a black-haired mermaid! Tuck your legs out of sight, I'll not disillusion her!'

She felt like laughing happily, but the thought of the house worried her.

'Is—is there anyone else there?'

'No. I don't keep open house for all my wards. One responsibility at a time is all I can handle!'

He pulled her closer to him, his smiling eyes looking into hers.

'Relax!' he ordered softly. 'Nobody is going to eat you. I want you right back to normal, seven years ago normal.'

'It was a long time ago,' she murmured, the smile dying. 'There's a lot of difference between fourteen and nearly twenty-two.'

'I noticed,' he assured her laconically and she was back to being aware of him again and it was not in any big brotherly manner. Being in Dan's arms was part of her dreams. The strong brown arms that held her close were sending painful shafts of excitement through her that brought colour to her face and a deep feeling of fright. There was now nowhere to hide from him, and the thought alarmed her. What had she been doing at Langford Hall but hiding from him? She was no more capable of dismissing him from her life than she had been four years ago. He was almost part of her.

Impulsively she turned her face into his strong, warm neck, as if she were a small animal hiding its head, but he said nothing at all. Soon she was lowered to the ground as she heard his feet step from the softness of a lawn to the hard wood of a veranda.

She opened her eyes to find herself being watched curiously by a woman with the roundest face she had ever seen—the darkest face, too—and she knew at once that this was Josie. The smile that came winging out to Anna, though, as the rather worried look of curiosity left Josie's face when she realised that Anna was not after all in a dead faint, brought a wholesome beauty to the dark face that warmed Anna instantly.

'Josie,' Dan introduced laconically. 'The very person who's about to tuck you up in bed!'

Anna wasn't really listening enough to protest, though; her eyes were skimming around the house as they walked inside, a happy-looking Josie bustling in front of them. It was a fabulous place, and there was no doubt at all that Dan was really rich, after all. Why she should have doubted it she could not fathom. Every one of his books had been a best seller and most of them were filmed.

'It could hardly be called a small bungalow,' she said ironically, and he laughed.

'No, but it's single-storeyed, no fuss or bother, no stairs to climb—simplicity.'

'Simplicity?' It looked as if he had been collecting art treasures for years: antiques, pictures, porcelain. It was beautiful! 'My goodness, what will you say, I wonder, if I break any of these ornaments?'

'Some punishment will be found,' Dan murmured darkly.

A man came into the house with some of their luggage, and this was Abe, Dan informed her. He was surprisingly tall and lanky after her view of his wife, and Anna just stood there, not at all recovered from a succession of surprises.

'Can I wander round and stare?' she asked.

'As soon as you've had a nice long drink,' Dan promised, taking her arm firmly and leading her back out to the cool veranda, sitting her in a white cane chair with comfortable bright cushions. 'You're looking a bit dehydrated.'

'You mean shrivelled?' She had a mischievous look and he smiled slowly.

'Ah! A sign of the old Anna surfacing. A few days' rest and you'll be back to normal.'

'Whatever that is,' Anna said thoughtlessly, leaning back and looking out over the colourful gardens to the clear green sea.

'Normal is when I look at you and say to myself, "That's Anna!" Irritating, beautiful and burning bright,' Dan said quietly. 'Until then you're just a little waif that I somehow managed to pick up and bring home.'

She didn't look at him, for there was a real danger that she would cry, but he ignored any sign of that, if he noticed. Josie was there almost at once with a long, cool, frosted drink that was like nectar.

'You now have about five minutes to wander around staring and breaking things,' Dan said briskly, pulling her to her feet when the drinks were finished. 'After that, a few hours' sleep.'

She didn't argue. She was feeling tired and strained, and this ridiculous urge to burst into tears was becoming much too strong. She shot him a grateful look and wandered off alone, leaving him to go into his study and sort out the mountainous quantity of writing he seemed to have done at Langford Hall. There was an air of almost burning satisfaction about him, and she knew he was thankful to be home. She would have to try and keep out of his way and let him go on as he normally did on his island.

She was just wandering back to the long, cool drawing-room when the telephone rang and she heard Dan answer it.

'Daphne, honey!' He sounded so delighted that Anna stopped in her tracks, an unwitting eavesdropper, her heart feeling like lead. 'I just got back not half an hour

ago! What? Oh, he does, does he? Put him on, then!'
She heard Dan's low laughter, and then words that she
would rather not have heard at all. 'Hello, Trevor! How's
my boy?'

She turned and fled blindly the way she had come,
almost crashing into Josie, who took one look at her
and led her straight to a cool, tranquil room where the
sheets of the bed were already turned back.

'Mr Dan says you gotta sleep, and I should just think
so!' she said in a quietly outraged voice, clucking away
as she manoeuvred Anna to the bed. 'Now you just slip
out of that dress, Miss Mazzini, and into bed with you!'

'I'm Anna,' she said tiredly, the tears too hot and dry
to fall.

'Right then, Miss Anna, let's get you into this bed!'

It was nice to be mothered, and Anna only wanted to
sleep; anything to forget the joy in Dan's voice on the
telephone. He hadn't married Daphne, but it made little
difference, for she was still there in his life, and his words
at Langford Hall took on a new meaning—'In the end,
we didn't fancy it.' Perhaps not. Many people in Dan's
sphere simply lived together. The joy in his voice had
told her all she needed to know. She was here, trapped,
and he was beginning to move back into her life.

He came quietly in as she was lying beneath the sheets,
her eyes still not closed.

'Anna? Josie said she found you staggering about
looking ready to collapse. Are you all right?'

'Just tired,' she whispered faintly, willing him out of
the door. 'I'll be all right when I've had a sleep.'

'Josie will wake you up later,' he told her softly,
coming to the bed and looking down at her. 'Just drift
off to sleep and try not to worry about anything.'

'I never got in touch with Bryan!' she said anxiously, clinging to her own little lie when everything had been dashed from her again.

'You can phone when you get up,' he said rather tersely, and she thought he was angry at her forgetfulness.

'It's too expensive!'

'Give me the number and I'll phone for you,' he offered coolly, but she couldn't let him do that. He might find out that it was not the great love-affair of the century.

'He—Bryan might be asleep. He works so hard that...'

'So we'll wake him up! If you phoned me when I was asleep...' He suddenly turned and walked to the door. 'You can do it later. Maybe he'll be on night shift then,' he finished sarcastically, and as he closed the door behind him the dry, hot tears spilled on to her cheeks. What was she doing here, living in Dan's house, beginning to dream impossible dreams? It was all so hopeless. It always had been.

She awoke to find a dark face close to hers, as Josie shook her gently and peered down at her.

'Time for dinner, Miss Anna,' she said quietly. 'Mr Dan thought you'd better wake up in case you couldn't sleep tonight.'

Sleep! It was the safest state to be in, but she nodded and smiled, swinging her legs out of bed and realising that she didn't feel so bad. The dreary feeling of lethargy that had dogged her for so long was gradually fading and, if in its place an actual pain had grown when she thought of Dan, at least she felt more alive. She showered

and looked in the wardrobe, where Josie had put her clothes.

One after another they looked far too big now, and after a while she chose a wrap-over dress of lemon that at least could be belted tightly and would not actually drop off. When she walked into the drawing-room, now softly lit, Dan turned from the drink he was pouring and his eyes moved over her slowly.

'Beautiful bones, glorious clouds of hair and very little else!' he said flatly. 'We'll have to fatten you up or we'll misplace you!'

He handed her a drink, grinning suddenly as she grimaced.

'Brandy for medicinal purposes,' he informed her. 'Watch it doesn't go to your head in your weakened condition. I'd hate to see you get merry and lose all that cool control.'

His eyes were intently on her face and she anxiously joked at once. 'And go around knocking those expensive ornaments to the ground?'

'I wasn't actually thinking of that kind of treasure,' he shot back at her with a quirk to his lips when she looked at him quickly.

Luckily Josie came in then to announce that dinner was served, and Anna was thankful to turn the conversation to more safe topics and listen to Dan as he talked about the islands.

Panic struck her again later, though, as Josie came in when they were sitting in the drawing-room with coffee. She had come to say goodnight and, incongruously, she was wearing a small white hat. Anna had to stifle laughter as she nodded her farewell.

'Does she go to bed in a hat?'

She was almost bursting with laughter, but Dan's reply wiped the smile from her face.

'Josie and Abe have finished for the day. They're going home. She always travels in style.'

'Home? They don't live in the house?'

'No.' Dan got up to pour more coffee. 'They live on one of the bigger islands a few miles away. That small launch by mine is theirs. I bought it for them. It was the only way I could get them to work here. The rules were that every night they went home. I had to agree, and I must confess it suits me.'

'Then who... I mean—we—we're alone here as soon as they go?'

'Yes.' He turned to look across at her. 'There's nothing to worry about. If you dream of pirates just shout out, I'll be there like a rocket!'

She hadn't meant that. It was bad enough being here with Dan when there was someone else. Now apparently they were alone on the island, and as she heard the sound of a launch leaving the small quay she felt a wave of near fright.

'What—what will people think?' she burst out.

'What people?' He came and looked down at her. 'You've been safe with me for so many years that I'm astonished you don't feel safe now.'

'I—I do! I was only thinking that people...' She couldn't say Daphne. She couldn't bring herself to even think the name evenly.

'Ah! You mean Bryan?' he said mockingly. 'But he doesn't know at all. Just don't enlighten him.'

'I—I don't keep secrets from Bryan.' Every defence was up; it was not that she feared Dan but that she feared herself.

He was towering over her, a strange feeling in him communicating itself to her without any words.

'He doesn't even know your whereabouts yet. Telephone him now. You did say he would be frantic.'

He sounded remarkably sardonic, as if he just didn't believe her, and she took the bull by the horns in sheer self-defence.

'I will, thank you, if you'll get me the number.'

'No sooner said than done!'

When he had the number ringing, he left her to it and closed the door behind him, to her great relief. Bryan wasn't frantic, he was simply astonished, and she had a good talk to him, longer than she would normally have done. It was just wonderful to hear a sane voice. She was beginning to think that she was anything but sane, and she had her suspicions about Dan's sanity. If Daphne should suddenly come... Not being married didn't mean a thing. Daphne had Dan's child, and if they decided to live together unmarried then it was no different, really. Dan belonged to Daphne, and she would be hurt and angry to find someone else here.

When she rejoined Dan he was not looking too pleased, and she felt guilty about the cost of such a call.

'I—I'm sorry I was so long. The time simply flew.'

'It's supposed to, when you're in love! I remember it so well.' He suddenly relented, smiling at her and opening the door. 'Let's stroll on the beach before bedtime,' he suggested. 'There's a great moon tonight. We'll look for pirate ships!'

They walked quietly on the beach in the silvery moonlight, but she was still as tight as ever inside, and nothing that Dan said did anything to relax her. He left her at

the door of her room, but came slowly just inside as he watched her walk away from him.

'When you're back to your normal weight we'll take a trip to Nassau and get you a few things to wear,' he informed her quietly. 'Not much use in rigging you out in the wrong size. I presume you don't always intend to stay as you are? You do intend to gradually eat more than you did at dinner?'

'I won't need any more clothes!' Anna protested quickly.

'Of course you will! I fly to the studios from time to time, and regularly drop over to Nassau for dinner at night. Naturally you'll come with me.'

'I won't be here that long!' She swung round on the edge of panic, thinking of meeting Daphne and Dan's little son. Did Daphne know that she was here? Had he told her when she'd phoned earlier? What would she think? After all, she wasn't Dan's sister!

'How do you intend to leave?' Dan asked quietly, and he must have been joking, although there was no smile on his face.

'You've kidnapped me?'

She joked too, but the smile remained only tentative as he said evenly, 'Yes.'

'I wish you wouldn't make such scary jokes, Dan!' She gave a rather desperate little laugh, but he just stood watching her, his eyebrows raised, the tawny eyes very wide open.

'Who's joking?' he asked softly, then walked out, closing the door on her as she started the trembling that came on a wild and burning wave of excitement. It was,

of course, ridiculous, but his face had looked so serious... She got into bed, shivering in spite of the soft warmth of the night.

CHAPTER FIVE

WITHOUT any orders or suggestions, Dan seemed to have set up a regime for her total recovery. It was foolproof. During the day he worked and ignored her. He was in his study before she got up, and he stayed there, the sound of the typewriter warning her that he was not to be disturbed.

Josie treated Dan's work with almost religious fervour, even tiptoeing past the study when he was working. It finally began to amuse Anna, and she did the only things she could do. She rested, ate, wandered around the island and swam in the pool behind the house. Gradually her health returned, she became brown and she put on the much needed pounds. Dan made no comment, but at dinner each night his eyes would flare over her in a quick, intent inspection, and she would see the firm lips quirk in amusement as he noted her progress. He was the most cunning man she had ever known. She was still fighting to keep him out of her life, but it was hard, harder each day.

It dawned on her one morning after breakfast that there was no sound of work coming from the study, and when she went into the kitchen to enquire Josie told her why.

'Mr Dan, he's gone off to Nassau early on,' she said with a smiling complacency, her hands busy polishing the silver. 'He says not to wait lunch but he'll be back soon after.'

83

It made her feel slightly trapped, as if he really had kidnapped her, and she wandered restlessly about all morning until Josie served her lunch.

She was just finished when the launch came in, and Dan was soon striding into the room, his arms full of boxes.

'Did you miss me?' he asked brightly, with a quick flicker of amusement on his lips as he noted her rather sullen face.

'A trip out would have been nice!'

'I was shopping,' he announced, piling the boxes at the end of the table. 'I decided that you're coming along nicely and it's time you had more things to wear for our regular trips to Nassau for dinner, at least twice a week.'

'You shopped for clothes for me?' She didn't know whether to be delighted or severely annoyed. 'There's not much chance of a fit!'

'I had Josie look at the labels in your clothes for size, and I had the help of an old friend who owns a boutique. When we'd gone through her possible things that would suit, she went with me to the other shops and here we are. You're an ungrateful wretch, girl!'

He wasn't angry though, and he strode out, calling to Josie for a late lunch. Anna looked at the boxes with mixed feelings. What had he told his friend? Did he tell her that he had his sister staying? Did his friend know Daphne?

She was irresolute for a while, and then her desire to open the boxes won. She picked them up and staggered to her room, letting them tumble on to the bed and diving into the first one to hand. She couldn't have chosen better. It was a dream of a dress, almost the same colour as the dress she had worn as chief bridesmaid.

She held it in front of her and looked through the mirror, surprised to see that her colour was back to normal, her thin arms now merely slender. She looked well, she even looked happy! She swirled around, watching the dress flare with her, and Dan's burst of laughter from the open door had her flushing painfully.

He was leaning against the doorway, watching, his eyes so vividly alive that a quick flare of intense feeling shot through her.

'Oh, Dan, it's lovely!'

'So are you!' he said quietly. 'I'll never forget how you looked at the wedding. You'll wear that the first time we go to Nassau?'

'Oh, try and stop me!' she sang out, and he walked slowly in towards her.

'I wouldn't try to stop you no matter what you did,' he said softly. He stood there looking at her and she couldn't take her eyes from him. Her fingers curled around the dress and she took a great shuddering breath.

His eyes followed the movement of her fingers and he reached out, gently uncurling them, taking the dress and tossing it on to the bed. She stood still, her legs too weak to move, accepting it as fate when he reached for her as he had done once before, and cupped her face in his hands.

'Now what are you scared of?' he asked softly. His eyes flared over her face, his fingers gently massaging her nape and her eyes closed slowly. 'Nobody's going to hurt you, Anna,' he murmured.

He brushed his lips across her forehead and then he was gone, leaving her trembling and fighting a disappointment that was shame itself. She had wanted him to kiss her, her feelings hungry and uncontrolled. He hadn't

meant to, hadn't wanted to, and why should he? There was Daphne, his son, his own life here that she knew nothing of. Her own feelings were dangerous, and they were beginning to take over all her thoughts!

Gradually she became more settled. It was hard not to be settled with Dan. He was too much a familiar part of her thoughts to remain a stranger, and he worked too much to be a constant worry to her. She was not lonely, though. There was so much tranquillity here that loneliness was out of the question. It was a place that healed.

Although the island was only three miles square, there seemed to be a lot of it, and Anna walked over most of it after suitable warnings from Dan. The shoreline was the interest that drew her most; the fine white sand and the clear turquoise sea an endless delight. She wanted to see the secret underwater world, and although she never pestered Dan he seemed to know where she spent most of her time.

'I think you're about ready to try your hand at scuba diving,' he remarked one morning, coming to join her as she wandered in the rock pools, peering down at the miniature world of water with fascinated eyes.

'Now?' She couldn't keep the enthusiasm from her voice, and he grinned at her and nodded.

'Why not? I should have been more attentive to you, I know, but when a book is running well, I hardly know that anyone else is around.'

'I noticed!' Her rather dry rejoinder drew his eyes back to her face.

'You feel neglected? I gained the decided impression that you wanted to be left alone. You've become resigned to captivity?'

'You have a weird way of teasing,' she muttered in embarrassment, but he simply went on looking at her steadily.

'Teasing?' he murmured, his tawny eyes intent. 'What if I told you that I had no intention of letting you go?'

'I'd stow away on Josie and Abe's boat!' she snapped impatiently. 'Be serious, Dan! Can we dive now?'

'Sure!' It was his American connection coming out, and it immediately reminded Anna of Daphne and the little boy. The eager look died on her face and Dan looked at her quizzically.

'I offered to take you,' he protested. 'It was even my own idea, if you remember. Why the sulking, I can't imagine. Come on!'

He walked back towards the house and Anna followed more slowly. The delight had all gone out of it. It was so easy to forget everything when she was here. The mind only remembered the things that pleased it, that held no hurt.

He waited for her on the veranda and then led her to the back of the house. As to her supposed sulks, he ignored them. The equipment was stowed away indoors, to her surprise, and she felt less inclined to be miserable as Dan pulled out masks, cylinders and flippers.

'The bikini, I think,' he ordered, waving her off to her room as he began to check the air pressure in the two cylinders. When she came down, he was already coming back from the boat for a second load.

Josie appeared with a basket containing a packed lunch, and Anna took it excitedly, her eyes on Dan's face.

'Will we be out for long?'

Her voice was a little anxious; in fact, she felt a sudden uneasiness that contained more excitement than fear. Dan turned to look at her, looking almost immediately away.

'It depends upon how apt a pupil you are. If you can't master the technique we'll be straight back and we'll eat our lunch on the veranda.'

He was dismissive, as if she were a nuisance, and Anna's lips tightened angrily. Her expression merely gave him cause for a sardonic smile, and she settled herself in the white launch as he took the wheel and headed out to sea to make a swing around the island. She had expected to have to wade out from the shore, and the idea of going straight in off a boat was a little alarming, but after that derisive look she was not about to query anything at all.

When the boat finally stopped and Dan anchored in a tiny bay, Anna looked around in surprise. She had thought that in her wanderings she had covered all of Amara Cay, but she didn't recognise this place. There was no beach. The thick vegetation grew down to the water, hanging over it in many places, in others stopping at white, rocky outcrops like small cliffs. It was a very tranquil, secret place.

There was no time to gaze about, though. They had come to dive, and Dan immediately began to gear up. He was businesslike and brisk.

'Into this. I think it's going to fit!' He handed her a wetsuit, his eyes watchful as she struggled into it.

'Did you buy this on your shopping expedition?' she enquired nervously, speaking more to relieve the strain of his tawny eyes on her so intently than to find out where it had come from.

'No. It belongs to a friend of mine who likes to dive. She's not going to mind one bit.'

Daphne was the first thought in her mind, but it might not be. Dan's life-style might not preclude other women.

'Do you dive here? I—I mean—when she comes to stay...' There was a morbid desire to be told about her, to be told about any woman who came here. It made her feel childish, but she couldn't help asking.

'No. She's a good diver. We dive off Andros!'

'Will we go there when I know what to do?'

He was still simply staring at her, and she didn't know what else to do but ask foolish questions.

'You? Not likely! There's a deep water drop there. One thousand fathoms, to be exact. However good you get, you'll never go there!'

'I might get as good as your friend!'

He turned impatiently away and began to hitch a cylinder on to his back, not even answering. She noticed that he was not in a wetsuit. His black shorts and T-shirt were his only protection. His legs were strong and golden, the black shorts emphasising his lean hips. Her eyes roamed over him of their own free will, her cheeks flushing as she found him watching this appraisal.

'You're not wearing a wetsuit!' she said hastily.

'*I* know what I'm doing,' he assured her drily. 'Down there it's not quite so safe as on the deck. Don't touch anything unless I let you know that it's safe. You can be cut or burned by coral, and there are plenty of other things to either sting or cut you—sea urchins with spines, jellyfish sometimes. Just stick with me until you can recognise danger for yourself.'

Anna nodded solemnly and went on looking at him as he got ready.

'Does—does she stay at the house?' Her face was rosy with embarrassment, but the words just poured out by themselves.

'Naturally!'

He never asked her what she was talking about. He seemed to know that she was still deeply concerned with the previous conversation.

'Does she sleep in the room I have now?'

'You mean, does she sleep with me?' he asked coldly.

'I—I meant nothing of the sort!' Her face flushed wildly because she *had* meant that and he knew it.

'Then if you meant nothing of the sort, you'll not want an answer, will you?' He turned to her with the flippers and she bent to fix them, glad to be able to look away. When she straightened he was holding a cylinder and simply twirled his hand, indicating that she should turn away. She felt the weight on her shoulders as he slid the straps into place and came around to fasten it securely.

'Only the mask now!' He went to the side and looked over and then motioned her forward. 'I'll go over. You come down the ladder carefully and just wait as soon as you touch the water. Dip your mask in and then hang on until I tell you to move. All right?'

She nodded and looked away. She felt more uncomfortable, she felt lonely. With a few words he had distanced himself from her, all their new-found friendliness gone.

'There's nothing to worry about.' Dan's voice was suddenly softer, and his hand came to her arm.

'I'm not at all worried!' She looked determinedly at him and he nodded, and then he was just stepping off

the edge of the boat, allowing himself to fall backwards into the clear, dazzling water.

She could see him all the way down, his powerful body twisting as he kicked upwards, and she began what seemed to be a very tricky descent, quietly furious that she could not simply fall gracefully into the water like Dan. She wasn't about to try anything fancy, though. He had said there was deep water off Andros, and it looked deep enough here, even though she could see the white, sandy bottom.

'Right! Come to me!'

He was on the surface only a couple of yards away, and she found that the flippers were not the clumsy encumbrances in the water that they had been on deck. She floated across, gently kicking her feet, a slow smile beginning on her face as she felt the freedom of the water.

'No daring deeds,' Dan warned. 'Gently does it!'

He spent what seemed like ages teaching her to use the equipment, and then he sank away, looking up at her through his mask, the sunlight through the water turning his hair to burnished gold, his brown hand signalling, and she sank rather fearfully towards him, her mind rapidly running through his instructions.

It was fabulous! He moved slowly away, looking back every few seconds to make sure she was still following, and after a while she began to really enjoy herself. Now she was actually in the wonderland. The coral, like flowers, below her, brilliantly coloured fish all around. It was incomparably beautiful, and Anna forgot every anxiety, her only irritation that she could not talk excitedly to Dan at once.

After a long while he touched her arm, signalling her upwards, and she thought they were going back to the

boat, but in fact they were some way away from that. As she followed him he suddenly dived and she followed, finding herself in a spectacular underwater cave. Even here the strong sunlight penetrated, and as Dan rose to the surface she followed and found that they could hold their heads above water.

'Enjoying it?' He pushed his mask up and she followed suit, her face alight with excitement.

'Dan, it's fabulous! I could stay here forever.'

'You've got fifteen more minutes!' he laughed. 'Don't forget that. If you disobey, you'll be shorebound for good!'

'Spoil-sport!' She made a face and then added, 'Anyway, I'm starving!'

'That's the first sensible thing you've said since we left England. Let's get back to the launch!'

His hands came to her shoulders and he bent his head, his lips brushing hers quickly, and then he slid his mask over a quite impassive face and sank beneath the water.

It was a second before she could follow. The quick, light kiss only added to the magical feeling that there was nobody else in the world, and the shining, buoyant water was a mystical place where Dan was hers alone.

She saw him shoot upwards and followed, and then she was being helped to the hot, sunny deck, Dan's firm hands shedding her equipment for her, her shaking legs telling her that she was still not back to normal strength and that Dan had been quite right to ration her stay below.

They ate their lunch and then Anna spread out her towel and lay in the shadow of the deck-house, out of the fierce rays of sunlight that had dried her as she ate. Dan stayed in the sun, but he was darkly tanned, used

to this brightness, and she didn't want to get burned and ruin everything. He stayed hazily in her mind as she drifted to sleep, the gently rocking boat soothing her troubles away.

She awoke later to find him standing close, looking down at her.

'Oh, I never meant to sleep! Are we going back in the water?' She struggled up and he took her hand, pulling her to her feet.

'No. I think you've had enough for today. Tomorrow, if I can manage it. You did nothing wrong, nothing dangerous. We'll quit while we're ahead!'

'I didn't realise I was such a liability.' She looked up with an impish smile, her mind still partly in the mood of dreams, no barrier up between herself and Dan.

'You're not. I'm just in a cautious mood. Right now I feel I've moved carefully through a dangerous afternoon and come out relatively unscathed. Who knows, if we stay longer, a chickcharney may appear and do untold damage!'

'What's that?' Her face held the fascinated awe of childhood as she looked up into the amused eyes, and he became very serious.

'It's red-eyed and three-toed and it hangs from trees. Its sole function is to cause trouble!'

Amused exasperation flared across her face as she realised he was teasing. 'There's no such thing!'

'Don't be too sure. I thought there were no mermaids, but look how wrong I was!'

His eyes ran over her figure, now smoothly tanned, the black bikini merely an enticement, her lustrous black hair sun-dried and shining. Her skin felt as if he was

touching her, and she shivered as his eyes returned to hers.

His arm curled out, unexpectedly encircling her waist, pulling her forward as his hand collected her long black hair, a silken rope to twine around his wrist, his gentle pull forcing her head up until her face was close to his.

'Kiss me, mermaid,' he ordered huskily. 'I brought you from the sea, and now you owe me a wish!'

'Dan!' There was panic mixed with her laughter, but he waited, his lips hovering over hers, his arm drawing her close. For the first time in her life she felt Dan's skin against hers, and a gasp of excitement left her lips as forbidden feelings raced through her. Everything blanked in her mind, nothing left but feeling, dangerous, alluring awareness. Dan's eyes burning into hers, all laughter gone.

'Kiss me!' It was a faint whisper, the sound of the sea almost drowning it, the sound of her own heart pounding much louder, and her eyes moved to the long, firm lips that now looked sensuous and enticing.

'Anna!' Her name was a low sound deep in his throat, a husky order, and she closed her eyes, her trembling lips brushing his, opening when he suddenly deepened the kiss and released her hair, pulling her fully into his arms, moulding her against him.

He murmured deeply, a sound of male satisfaction that shot waves of heat through her whole body. The fright left her as she gave herself up to feeling, and her arms went tightly around his neck as his hands began to search her skin urgently, moving across her warm back, spanning her waist and the slender length of her thighs.

They might have been deep in the water or up in the sky; there was nothing but pleasure and warmth and a blind instinct to cling to him.

'You entrancing little devil!' His lips caressed her face and neck, his strong hands arching her against him. 'Don't move. Stay with me.'

It reminded her that they had to go back to the house, and it reminded her of her place here. The memory of Daphne and the small boy brought Anna out of the trance that she had willingly entered. She pulled away and turned her back, ashamed as she had never been.

'Anna?' His hands came to her shoulders, but he made no attempt to turn her to face him. She couldn't face him, and she felt him withdraw from her even before his hands had left her skin. 'I'm sorry. The sunlight is supposed to be an aphrodisiac. Clearly it is. Maybe I'd better get back to California after all!'

'It—it was my fault,' she confessed in a voice that held some measure of her shame. 'If I hadn't been . . .'

'If you hadn't been what—yourself?' he interrupted harshly. 'I can hardly think of anyone else you could be, so don't burden yourself with guilt. We both know what all this is about, all this underlying antagonism, all this bottled-in heat!'

Yes, she knew! It was her obsession with Dan, a child's love that had grown to a woman's desire, even though it disgusted her! As for Dan—wasn't he a man, after all? It had been a long time since he had felt only the need to protect her. The very thought brought tears to her eyes. What had he done but protect her when she was so ill at college? She was here because he was protecting her. It was a hopeless muddle, and every barrier

she had built up against him for over four years was crumbling daily.

'I should go home.' She said it as coolly as trembling lips would allow, her eyes on his golden, handsome frame as he bent over the wheel, his hand on the ignition.

'Right! I'll just spin us around and head out over the Atlantic,' he assured her sarcastically. 'It may make some sort of record!'

'I'm serious!'

'It felt like it,' he jeered. 'Unfortunately, it didn't last long enough for me to be quite sure. Maybe next time we can assess it better!'

'There won't be a next time!' Anna snapped, her trembling hand clutching the towel tightly.

'It's a small island, baby!' he reminded her mockingly. 'You're on it and so am I. Poor Bryan is miles away, dedicated to science. It will happen again, it's been boiling long enough!'

He started the engine, ignoring her and she sat abruptly, her legs unsteady, her mind not at all sure what she had heard. He was keeping her here until she…until they…

The boat moved out and turned for the other side of the island, and she walked forward urgently to stand by him, looking up into his face as he stared out to sea.

'Let me go home!' she demanded, her voice tight and afraid.

'No!'

He didn't even look at her. His face was cool and remote, and she knew he had never had the slightest intention of letting her go. She didn't know him at all. The Dan she had known was gone, a frightening, exciting stranger taking his place.

'Dan!'

'Save yourself an argument,' he said harshly. 'I'm not letting you go!'

Of course it couldn't go on. She knew it couldn't, although Dan behaved as if nothing had happened at all. It had happened to her, though. She had come to excited life, her conscience weakening daily, her eyes constantly on Dan.

She went everywhere with him; she had no choice. At least twice a week they went to Nassau to dine, and danced until very late. At first she had been anxious, afraid when he touched her, but she was always reduced to trembling acquiescence when those eyes smiled into hers and his hand reached out to take her own. For all her fears and guilt, it was just an excuse to be in Dan's arms, and she prayed he wouldn't realise it. It was only a dream, and she acknowledged that. It seemed to merely amuse him.

Often they visited other islands during the day, when Dan would suddenly declare he had worked for long enough, the white launch skipping over the sea and nosing its way into new and exciting places. Away from Nassau there were no crowds, everything was relaxed and laughter came easily. He told her fantastic tales of the Out Islands, many of which were hard to believe, and the islanders who talked to them were even worse.

Anna sat on the low stone wall of the harbour after a day looking around Cat Island. She was getting to know how Dan's mind worked, and she ate juicy pine-apple, her eyes amused as he coaxed an old Bahamian into talking. He was gathering material for a book, she

was sure, and the old man had no idea that his remi-
niscences were being directed.

He shot off at a tangent and Dan's eyes lost their intent
concentration as Anna became the focus of attention.

'It's the sweetest pineapple in the islands that's grown
here!' the old man said proudly, his eyes satisfied at her
enjoyment. 'We got everything!' He began a long reci-
tation on bush medicine that almost choked her with the
need not to laugh. She had never known there could be
so many aches or internal disorders, or so many
revolting-sounding cures.

She was only free to laugh when the old man had gone,
and Dan turned glittering eyes on her.

'What a pity I didn't know about all that,' he said
with teasing regret. 'I could have brought you over here
as soon as we reached the Bahamas, and you would have
been right as rain immediately!'

'Or poisoned!' Anna laughed.

'He never said anything about *obeah*!' Dan told her
seriously, getting her interest at once.

'*Obeah?* What's that?'

'Witchcraft. It's still practised here by the older people,
although they don't talk about it. They might have
opened up to you though, considering the way you look
with all that long black hair. Think what you could do
with a few potions.'

'I could have tried them out on Bryan!' she said
quickly, knowing perfectly well what potions he was
mocking about.

'Bryan? Who's he?' Dan asked softly, and all the
laughter was gone as suddenly as it had come. She had
to ignore it. She couldn't cope when he was like this.

'My fingers are sticky,' she complained fretfully, looking round for her bag.

'Lick them,' Dan murmured.

Before she could move he had taken her hand in his, lifting her slender fingers to his lips, drawing them into the warmth of his mouth.

'Don't!' Her whole body leapt as if she had been touched by an electrical charge, and she snatched her hand away, searching frantically for her handkerchief.

'Merely trying to oblige,' he assured her softly, taking her arm and leading her off towards the boat as if nothing at all had happened. Maybe it hadn't, for him! For her, it was just one more step along the way, one more thing to fire her wild obsession with him.

There was always the sound of his voice, deep and soft, and she sunned herself in the sound of it as the days drifted by. Sometimes he would be quiet, suddenly and unexpectedly, and then their eyes would meet, his tawny eyes taking on a deep glow as he seemed to read what was on her mind.

The trips to Nassau became almost like a drug, a burning need to be in his arms, and as they returned Dan would often be silent, leaving her to walk alone up to the house, then going to his study to work for hours, his face strained next day. It was becoming more difficult to be natural, and often she thought that he was deliberately forcing the tension up. It was a thrill that ran through the days, a force that was dragging her under.

CHAPTER SIX

ANNA waited each day as Dan worked, and never asked again to go home. Maybe he *had* kidnapped her! She didn't care. She lay like a contented cat beside the pool, her body almost sensuous as she thought of Dan. Each day the feelings inside her grew stronger. Each day their eyes held for just a little longer. She stretched sinuously, a smile on her face that was pure sensuality, her eyes opening to see Dan standing there watching her.

Colour flooded her cheeks, but she looked straight back and saw an answering flare of colour on his high cheekbones. Their eyes locked and she knew that his hands were slowly clenching and unclenching. She refused to look away because at that moment there was a madness in her, a need to fight for him, to keep him for herself. Her legs were turning to water and he took a step towards her, an acknowledgement of her feelings deep in his eyes.

It scared her and she tore her gaze away, knowing that she had been deliberately calling to him with her eyes and that this time he had been only too ready to respond. There was now no mockery on his face, only a raw, masculine need that was almost aggressive. She shot to her feet and raced towards the house.

'I think I'll change and go for a walk!'

She just flung the words over her shoulder, fully aware of what she was deliberately inviting. If he followed her she was too vulnerable to even make any protest. He did

not, and she knew he would have come to his senses and be feeling angry with himself and with her. Life had become too difficult. She spent all her days wanting Dan to touch her, and all she was doing was inviting disaster.

She sat on the edge of her bed, trying to feel the surge of disgust with herself that had protected her so far, but it would not come. Dan knew how she felt! He could hardly not. As she finally came rather fearfully back when she had changed, she could hear the hammering of his typewriter from behind the closed door of his study. What was he thinking? Was he angry with her, disgusted? She knew she should insist on going back to England, but she couldn't bring herself to say the words. It would mean that she would never see him again. Her teeth bit into her bottom lip and she almost jumped out of her skin as Josie followed her out on to the veranda, waving a letter.

'You got mail, Miss Anna! You got mail from England at last!'

It was a fat brown envelope, a big one, and it seemed to contain more than one letter. Clearly it had been posted on. She went back to her room to open it and sat on the bed, her heart still unsteady from her encounter with Dan.

A letter from Bryan fell out and she looked at it without opening it, her mind only seeing him hazily, because everything in life was a hazy dream now that she was here. This place was the vibrant reality. But her heart gave a quite alarming leap when the next letter that fell out had the college stamp on it.

This was it! She hardly dared open it. In the joy and excitement of being with Dan, she had completely forgotten her finals and the state she had been in at that

time. She read it slowly, read it again, and then she was on her feet, running to Dan with no thought but to share her happiness.

He looked up in surprise as she burst into his study, but she was riding on the crest of a wave. Only the stillness of his face, the forbidding look, brought her to her senses.

'I've got some mail from England!' she began breathlessly, the letter open in her hand.

He didn't even glance at it.

'A letter from Bryan,' he said sardonically, 'and you brought it for me to read? How kind!'

Disappointment clouded her eyes and she looked at him reproachfully. 'I passed my finals. I thought you might like to know.'

He got up slowly, a smile growing in his eyes, and came round the desk to her as she stood in the doorway. It dawned on her that she shouldn't be here at all. It was the inner sanctum.

'I'm sorry I burst in,' she began, but she couldn't keep it up. He was smiling, sharing her joy. 'Oh, Dan, I passed!'

'How?' He was standing in front of her, watching her face, and she grinned up at him.

'I got a *first*!'

She flung her arms around his neck, forgetting everything else, the letter waving in her hand, and his arms closed tightly round her, almost lifting her off her feet.

'I expected nothing less!'

'But I was in such a mess!' She drew back and looked up into his face, her arms still around his neck. 'The figures were sometimes almost a jumble. I don't know how I did it.'

'Witchcraft!' he suggested softly, his eyes gleaming into hers. 'Isn't that how you do everything?'

All at once she saw the look on his face, and the memory of the few seconds beside the pool flooded her mind. She was back in his arms as she had been on the boat. For whatever reason, she was here, being held tightly, Dan's face close. Her body softened almost instinctively and his eyes moved to her parted lips, his gaze almost caressing, when she looked up his eyes were half closed, his face tightening as his hand reached out to close the door. Then he was urging her gently back against it, his gaze locked with hers.

'Anna!' he said thickly as his lips closed over hers. He moved against her, his hands holding her face up to his. 'Anna!' She heard him repeating her name almost feverishly, and she became molten, arching against him as his hands moved to trace her spine and force her even closer.

It was part of her dreams—dreams of four years ago, dreams of now—and no other thought was in her head but Dan and his kisses, his hands moving over her, caressing her with growing heat. His lips left hers to trace her face, her neck, and she flung back her head, being anything he wanted, no subterfuge left.

His breathing was harsh and uneven, and the wild kisses she frantically placed against his skin did nothing to slow him down. He kissed her hungrily until her legs trembled and her mouth burned, until they were both gasping for breath, until she was ready to sink to the floor.

It was only Josie's knock on the door that brought any sanity to either of them.

'Mr Dan!' she called urgently. 'I think we got visitors!'

At first the words didn't penetrate their minds. Dan's lips and hands were busy exploring her, his mouth hotly nuzzling her skin, his fingers impatiently invading the neckline of her dress, but Josie called again.

'Mr Dan!'

'All right!' His voice was slurred and distant, and Anna's trembling body was only upright because he held her.

They looked at each other with dazed eyes, eyes that were gradually returning to sanity as realisation dawned on both of them. He let her go with obvious reluctance, standing close as she bent to pick up her letter with hands that shook uncontrollably.

Obviously she and Dan were not safe to be let out! It was her own behaviour at the pool that had brought this on again, that and her suddenly throwing herself into his arms.

'Anna, don't be embarrassed! It was a perfectly natural thing to happen. You're not my sister, after all. We have every right to kiss each other!'

'No, we don't,' she said tremblingly. 'I'm sorry. I forced all that to happen. I—I looked at you like that at the poolside and I threw myself at you and—and I quite forgot that I'm a big girl now with obligations!' she finished with a strained little laugh.

For a second he was silent, and when he spoke it was quietly savage, all the more so because his chest was still heaving with the effort of controlling such passion.

'An obligation called Bryan Scott? I forgot about him! Are you like that with him? Do you catch fire in his arms?'

She turned to him blindly, her head shaking without her even being aware of it, but he was not at all appeased. His anger was wild.

'You want me! You've wanted me for years and we both know it! Write and tell Bryan that! Tell him that you're more than ready when I kiss you. Tell him that you're begging for it daily, every time I look at you! Write to him! Confess your sins!'

He opened the door and strode out, clearly going to see who was coming in on the strange launch that they could now hear.

He had forgotten about Bryan? He had forgotten about *Daphne*, and so had she! She hadn't even cared. She was one of these people who broke couples up! She had plenty of sins to confess, because it was all her fault, her dangerous obsession with Dan, a lifetime's obsession. Was it Daphne coming in on the launch? Did Dan now see his son sitting beside her?

She raced to her room, guilt drowning the waves of fire that still raced over her skin. She could never face Dan again!

She had to, though. Josie came to her room about five minutes later, and almost leapt in after her quick knock on the door.

'Pretty yourself up, Miss Anna,' she babbled excitedly. 'We got company, a real—live—*film star*! Quick, honey, let me help you get ready. You look as if you've been dragged through a hedge!'

It was like being dressed by a steam-roller, but Anna was in no doubt that Josie had orders from Dan, and she went reluctantly to the veranda, following the sound of voices, her head still tingling from the rather violent ministrations of the hairbrush in Josie's strong hands.

There were three newcomers, and it wasn't difficult to spot the film star—it was Anita Sharp. Anna had seen her in a couple of films, and although she didn't look quite so glamorous in real life she was still a very beautiful woman, a presence. The other two were men, an older man with glasses and white hair, and a man who looked younger than Anita Sharp, but with a polish about his appearance that suggested he too was part of the world of the screen.

'A stowaway?' Anita's voice was edged with surprise. 'Dan, darling, I thought that nobody was allowed here except on business? Ah, I know, a secretary!'

'Anna is my ward!' Dan corrected swiftly, his eyes avoiding Anna. 'She's recuperating from illness.'

'You're her guardian? Darling, how utterly amusing! It takes some believing.'

'Believe it or not, as you please,' Dan said caustically. 'I don't much care. In fact, I'll correct that—I don't give a damn!'

'Oh, I believe you, only I did wonder why you were so slow at coming out to meet the launch,' Anita remarked mockingly, her sharp eyes on Anna, no doubt noticing her quick flare of colour.

'We were reading a letter! Anna has just passed her finals, her college exams,' he rasped, as Anita raised extravagantly puzzled eyes to both of them.

'Ah, I see! What were you studying, dear? Your colleges are different from ours, aren't they?'

'She was doing pure maths, at Oxford!' Dan informed her with a growing annoyance that she totally ignored. She wasn't used to this, but she seemed to be pretty thick-skinned. Anybody could see that Dan was ready to explode with rage.

'I think you'd better watch your tongue, Nita!' the older man growled with a quick smile at Anna. 'You're in the presence of a very bright young lady here. They don't take dummies at Oxford.'

'Did you get a good pass?' The younger man was looking keenly at Anna, and when he spoke she suddenly realised that he at least was English.

'A first.' She shrugged in a wave of embarrassment. She could well have done without this interest from the visitors. She had problems aplenty, and they were all her own.

'Wow! Will you help me with my tax returns?'

A real human being! Anna returned his cheerful grin thankfully, and sat uneasily at the very edge of one of the chairs.

'Break out the champagne, Dan!' Anita insisted, her eyes going from the two to Dan, who stood looking tight-lipped and angry. 'Surely you were going to celebrate the exam results? You can turn it into a double celebration as we've arrived!'

'I don't know that Dan will feel like celebrating extra work,' the older man said, but Dan was already looking in the cabinet just inside the door leading to the veranda, opening the lower cupboard.

'I have some already on ice for a celebration,' he murmured. 'This is as good a celebration as any!'

He got out glasses and the younger man strolled to Anna's side.

'Kieron Amery!' he offered, holding out his hand. 'I'm playing opposite Anita in the new film—Dan's last book. We've got a few points to cover and it's a good excuse to get away from the studio. Sorry if we're intruding.'

'You're not,' Anna said quickly, reminding herself that the guilty always felt very vulnerable. 'Who is the other visitor?' she asked in a lower voice.

'The producer, Dean Orton. He usually produces Dan's work.'

She knew that. She had seen the exciting films that were made from Dan's books. At any other time she would have been very interested to meet them, but not now. She had too many problems. At least with them in the house she could avoid Dan until she could get away, and she knew that she *had* to get away.

He came over with her champagne, and Kieron wandered over to Anita, who was giving him very sharp looks. It was obvious that she didn't like having another female present, and he was too astute not to play up to her. She could make life very awkward for a rising actor.

'I didn't realise you had champagne ready to celebrate my pass,' Anna murmured, unable to think what to say to Dan now.

'I didn't,' he informed her in a low, cool voice. 'The celebration I had in mind was something entirely different!'

His eyes held hers, probing and intent but angry, aggressively masculine, not Dan at all; and she felt her colour rising again.

'I'm sorry,' she said quickly, adding crossly. 'What a waste!'

'I have more champagne,' he murmured softly. 'It will keep.'

There was little doubt of what he meant, and she looked away swiftly, her blushes apparently angering him more.

A little while later she was cut out of things as the conversation turned to the studio, the changes needed and the battle about whether or not the script should be altered. Anna was glad to be able to slide off; only Kieron seemed to notice her departure. She stayed safely in her room, not knowing whether to pray for them to go or long for them to stay.

Anita Sharp was trouble; it was there in her eyes, in the confident way she monopolised Dan and expected the others to just wait until she had time to attend to them. Did Dan know her well? He must do. Jealousy began to gnaw at Anna, and she impatiently paced about. Daphne was the one who had cause for that! She had no rights at all as far as Dan was concerned.

He knocked on her door later to announce that they were all going out to dinner, his face clouding with anger when Anna said that she would stay and have dinner here.

'You'll come with us if I have to tuck you under my arm!' he rasped.

'I don't want to come. You can stay there and say your goodbyes. I'll only be in the way!'

'They're not going anywhere,' Dan snapped. 'They'll be back here later and they're staying for two days. We have to thrash this thing out, and I'm damned if I'm leaving Amara Cay to go to the studios!'

'I still don't see why I should...' Anna began, but he turned angrily to leave and just growled at her.

'Get dressed to dine in Nassau or I'll be back and dress you myself!'

'Dan!' Her urgent voice stopped him and he turned at the door, his eyes narrowed and cold. 'Dan, I want to leave. I want to go back to England!'

'No!' He just said the one word and she stared at him in horror.

'What do you mean—no? I want to go home.'

'You're missing Bryan?' he jeered, coming back towards her, and the only description of the way he moved that she could think of was prowling. There was a menace about him that she had never seen in Dan, but she was annoyed and really desperate to get away. She stood up to him, her dark eyes blazing.

'I want to go home. I'm *going* home. Tomorrow!'

'And I said no. I meant just that!'

'Have—have you gone mad?'

His eyes too were blazing, and she found herself backing away, a fact that seemed to give him some satisfaction.

'Quite probably,' he conceded. 'However, mad or not, no is no and that's just what I mean. You're going nowhere!'

He turned and walked away, and her breath came out in one thankful gasp. She had been holding it for the past few seconds.

'There'll be an even bigger gasp of breath than that if you're not ready to dine when I call for you!' he threw at her as he left.

She didn't doubt for one minute that he meant it. Dan was walking on the knife-edge of desire. She recognised it because that was exactly what she was doing herself.

She wore the rose-silk dress, and Kieron Amery gave a low whistle as she walked into the drawing-room later. Only the men were there. Anita was using her woman's prerogative and keeping them waiting.

'Now, if I had a ward like you I would never leave home!' Kieron said with a laugh that brought a quick frown to Dan's cool face.

'She'd wipe the floor with you at chess and utterly demoralise you!' Dan said ironically, but Kieron just grinned at her and she found herself smiling back. She was still smiling when Anita made her grand entrance, and the fact that she was talking to Kieron didn't endear her to Anita at all. What with Dan's glowering looks and Anita's quick, darting glances, she was glad to go out to the launch. Even there Kieron sat down beside her and kept up a flow of conversation that monopolised her attention for the whole trip. She was very grateful to him, but perfectly certain that he was treading dangerous waters.

Anita's temper was somewhat restored by the reception she got as they entered the dining-room of the hotel and people recognised her. She was not terribly amused though, that they recognised Dan, too, and her chagrin brought a secret smile to Anna's face.

She felt more normal than she had done for weeks. It was laughable to see a grown woman so desperate for attention. It also dawned on her that when Dan had brought her to Nassau they had avoided the bigger hotels that were haunted by tourists. Now she knew why. He liked privacy. He was not particularly amused when he was asked to sign people's dinner napkins. Anna was bubbling over with laughter. It was barely held in check.

'If Anita doesn't kill you, Dan will!' Kieron murmured to her after one look at her face. 'I think we'd better dance. I feel like saving your life.'

'It's so funny!' Anna said as they went out on to the crowded floor and began to dance. 'There's Anita

bursting with pride, and Dan just about ready to explode with anger, all for the same reason.'

She began to laugh aloud and Kieron grinned down at her.

'Haven't you seen it happen with Dan before? He's often on television in the States.'

'He's just Dan to me,' she said quietly, the laughter dying away as she realised just how far apart they really were, worlds away, except for this desire. 'His family have taken care of me all my life. When his father died, the responsibility was just passed on to Dan. I can't think of him with a flashy life-style. He's just like a big brother.'

What a lie, she thought! Dan was something else altogether now. She loved him in an entirely different way, wanted him more each day, and the danger could only grow if he refused to let her go away.

He danced by with Anita, and some instinct of self-preservation surfaced in Kieron.

'Care to change partners, Dan?' he asked with a sultry look at Anita that made her preen.

'If you insist!' Dan took Anna into his arms with a show of reluctance that reminded her of his rage with her before they left the house, but it quite restored Anita's temper. With two men dancing attendance she was momentarily happy.

Dan was stiff and unsmiling, looking over Anna's head, watching the other dancers and completely ignoring her.

'We don't have to dance!' she said coldly. 'I've had enough, anyway.'

He just ignored her and pulled her closer, and she kept her eyes firmly on his white shirt, not daring to look up.

'For a person so skilled in mathematics, it's taking you a long time to count three buttons,' he murmured ironically. 'Maybe you should count with your fingers.'

He took her hand and raised it to his chest as his face brushed her hair.

'One, two, three,' he said softly, his hand guiding hers down the row of buttons to the steady beating of his heart.

'Please, Dan!' she whispered frantically, her hands beginning to shake.

'Please, Dan!' he jeered softly against her ear. 'Am I supposed to go on treating you like a little sister when you've been in my arms?'

'You—you mustn't talk like that!' She was beginning to tremble, her heart taking on a frightening rhythm, but he was utterly ruthless.

'Why? Doesn't Bryan talk like that? Do I shock your prim little academic mind? How academic is it when those big dark eyes look at me?'

She pulled away and stared at him, white-faced. He was quite different. Not Dan at all.

'I don't even know you now,' she said with a look that was unknowingly tragic.

'You've not known me for a long time. Seven years, to be exact,' he said tersely. 'You're still swinging between little girl and the fact that you want me!'

'I—I don't. It's not true!'

'It *is* true,' he insisted vibrantly, his hands punishingly tight on her narrow waist. 'You fight it because you feel guilty about your poor hard-working doctor, but he's not here, I am! You spend every day waiting for me to take you!'

She just stared at him, unable to say that it wasn't true. It *was* true and Dan was different. He didn't feel one drop of remorse about anything. If she accused him of being permanently attached to another woman, he would simply say the same thing: she was here and Daphne was not.

'I want to go home!'

He smiled slowly, his grip on her waist tightening, his thumbs probing her ribcage softly and suggestively.

'What a short memory you have, Anna,' he taunted. 'I won't let you go home. Surely you know that?'

They weren't dancing any more and people were beginning to take an interest in them. She pulled away and walked off the floor, and Dan followed. For the rest of the evening she didn't look at him. He frightened her. For the first time in her life she was scared of Dan, but even more scared of herself.

Fortunately, Dan was extremely busy. He spent hours with Dean Orton, thrashing out the small but tricky changes to the screenplay. Anna noticed that they all seemed to revolve around Anita, and she wondered just how much the woman's pushing had brought this about. It kept Dan away from her, though, and that was all to the good. Unfortunately, it also restricted her activities. It wasn't possible to be quite so free and easy with strangers in the house, and Anita's constant need for attention soon wiped the admiring grin off Josie's face.

'That woman can't do one single thing for herself!' she confided to Anna. 'Her bedroom looks like a hurricane hit it every day. She never even picks up the clothes she drops on the floor.'

'Soon they'll be gone, Josie. If you want any help, I'll be glad to help.'

Josie declined, but Anna had so little to do that she felt it her duty to help, and took to getting up to help with breakfast and, as often as not, washing the dishes after each meal. It gave her something to do, and a reason for sliding out of the room each evening.

When Dan found out, he was furious. She was just finishing off and Josie had gone home when Dan walked into the kitchen.

'What the hell are you doing?' he grated.

'Only helping. It's a lot of extra work for Josie. I used to help Edna at home.'

'In a rather different climate,' he reminded her testily. 'If Josie's overworked, than Abe can come in and help.'

'He does! You wouldn't get a meal if he didn't. If he didn't help, Josie and Abe would never get home.'

'She's quite used to having visitors come.' Dan's fury seemed to be dying out a little and he simply looked curious. 'I can't see how this group makes all that much difference.'

'Apparently Anita is a whole group by herself,' Anna retorted. 'You had no idea I was helping. It's quite possible that your other female visitors helped Josie without you even knowing.'

'That's true,' Dan said thoughtfully. 'Perhaps you'd better just carry on, after all.'

'And perhaps you could help Anita pick up her clothes from the bedroom floor!' Anna snapped, infuriated by his attitude and his ready acknowledgement that there had been women here.

'I'll see what I can do.' He turned to the door and Anna turned back to the sink and the dishes, her

shoulders tight with temper. Maybe he helped Anita to throw her things *on* the bedroom floor.

'Temper all gone now?' Dan's arms came round her from behind and she jumped with the sudden shock. 'Actually, you're safer here in the kitchen than being in the drawing-room,' he admitted. 'The battle is raging there. I'm just about ready to kill Anita.'

He bent his head and brushed his lips along her nape, his arms tightly around her. Anna struggled to get away but he spun her round, pressing her back against the sink, his hand tilting her chin.

'Peace, Anna?' he suggested disarmingly. 'I find it very hard to keep up any battle with you. Will you pull down the skull and crossbones? Hmm?'

He was smiling at her and she found her lips quirking. It was sheer madness, but she loved him so much that she just couldn't find any way to keep up the tight atmosphere between them.

'Oh, sorry! I'm interrupting something!'

Anita was upon them before either of them could move, and Dan merely turned slowly, his arm still around Anna.

'Not really,' he said glibly. 'I was just telling Anna that I'm taking everyone scuba diving tomorrow.'

'Oh, darling, count me out!' Anita said with a shudder. 'I can't stand those beastly little fish. I've got a fearful headache,' she added, looking at Anna. 'I wonder if there's any water for my tablet.'

'The tap is full of it,' Anna said with a sweet smile. 'Help yourself.'

Dan walked out of the room whistling under his breath, his grin only just hidden, and Anna walked out in the opposite direction. It was clear that Dan was quite

accustomed to covering his tracks deftly. She should be given a shaking for letting him get round her so easily.

She hadn't heard the last of Anita. She decided to walk along the beach. The moon was still bright, making everything like day, and she draped a jacket round her shoulders and walked out of the back door to avoid the others. Dan, it seemed, was once again shut in his study with Dean Orton, but as she came down the side of the house she heard voices on the veranda. Anita and Kieron. She stopped, scared they would hear her and ask her to join them.

'There's something going off between Dan and that little ward of his!' Anita remarked. 'He looks at her like a hungry wolf.'

'Don't be so disgusting, darling,' Kieron muttered. 'In any case, she's not his sister, as you know perfectly well, so what if there is?'

'Whatever it is, she's not here to recuperate, I can tell you that!' Anita announced. 'It's my belief that we interrupted something pretty torrid.'

'Nita! One of these days somebody is going to either sue you or murder you! She's only just finished at university and she's in Dan's care. I can quite see that she's been ill. She's still a little too thin.'

'I've seen you looking her over,' Anita said with a brittle laugh. 'Don't get interested, though. I found them in the kitchen in each other's arms. Does that dampen your ardour?'

'You're really too much!' He apparently had the temerity to be really annoyed with her. 'You know how he feels about Daphne. Then there's the boy!'

'So? He wouldn't be the first man to play around while he's waiting for a woman to make up her mind.'

Anna fled back to the house and her room. If she had wanted her suspicions confirmed, then this was it. Daphne had refused to marry Dan; they hadn't thought better of it, *she* had! Maybe Daphne knew that he played around. He had never denied that there were other women who came to Amara Cay, other women who stayed here when Josie and Abe went home. She felt sick inside, sick with herself and with Dan.

CHAPTER SEVEN

THE NEXT day Dan seemed to be busier than ever. Anna was back to the tight restraint and he noticed at once, his own face clouding in anger. He took it out on Anita. If the alterations were for her benefit, then she certainly was not about to get off without some work. The drawing-room become a studio for the better part of the morning and she was kept hard at it, Kieron feeding her the new lines. Anna helped an unusually bad-tempered Josie and then escaped to the beach after lunch. Scuba diving, it seemed, was definitely off.

She was none too pleased when Kieron and Anita finally made their escape and joined her. Not only did she now know what they thought, but Kieron was looking at her in an entirely different way, a speculating look that made her uncomfortable and embarrassed. For the first time ever she was worried about being in her black bikini. His eyes never left her, and when Dan and Dean came out to join them she wandered off further along the shining sands. Irritation flared over her when she noticed that Kieron had changed his position to be able to see her still. She marched back to the house, determined to dress and stay indoors.

She met Josie as she was going to her room, and she was too late to hide her expression.

'You coming indoors on this lovely day, Miss Anna?'

'I'm going to change. I don't think I'm wearing enough clothes!' she added with a burst of unusual an-

noyance. She never spoke like that to Josie, and the dark face was instantly thoughtful. The knowing look in the dark eyes made Anna wonder if Josie had been looking out of the window, or if Abe had been in with a few words of gossip.

'Now what you want is a nice wrap to cover most of you!' Josie assured her. 'I got something!'

She darted away and was back from the kitchen almost at once, a length of silky material in her hands that she held up for Anna to see.

'You got black hair like the girls here,' she pointed out. 'It sure is pretty and so long. We bought this for you last night at the market. All that help, and you just getting better. We wanted to give you a little present.'

'Oh, Josie! How kind!'

Anna didn't know what to say. It was so unexpected, and her eyes moved over the material in admiration. It was brilliantly coloured: bright flowers of red and blue on a cream background. She wasn't sure what she could make with it, but it was really beautiful.

'Well, I didn't know what to get, but Abe chose this. That man's a real romantic!' Josie laughed, her whole body shaking. 'I'll show you how it works.'

She wrapped it around Anna's waist, tying it in a knot, a great deal of satisfaction on her face as she stepped back to look. It came to Anna's ankles, a brilliantly coloured sarong, and Josie's face was filled with glee.

'You just want a big flower in your hair and you'll look like one of them island girls!' she said suggestively. 'You're better than any *film star*!'

As their eyes met, Anna saw a look of mischief in Josie's eyes that at first stunned her and then brought a little smile to her lips. It was 'get your own back' time

as far as Josie was concerned, and she felt that she had better go back to the beach before Josie called to Abe to make her go back.

She walked out on to the veranda, the silk brushing her legs and blowing softly in the breeze, and she stopped to pick a hibiscus from the bush by the door, tying the bright crimson flower against the blue-black shine of her hair. It just touched the creamy texture of her lightly tanned skin, and she glanced round questioningly to find Josie standing in the shadows, her white grin stretching across her face.

She wandered nonchalantly back, skirting the others and walking down to the sea, but she could almost hear the atmosphere and she kept her face turned away, her own grin threatening to equal Josie's. It wasn't long before Kieron joined her, his eyes wide with admiration.

'You look as if you've escaped from Hawaii!' he said, his eyes running over her from head to foot.

'I was beginning to feel that my legs were burning!' she answered drily.

She didn't want Kieron's company. He was not the easy-going companion now that he had been before. Now that he had heard Anita's poisonous words, his look was entirely different, and she was hard pressed not to speak to him sharply and send him packing. Josie deserved some help though in her attempt to put Anita in her place, and Anna could see Anita boiling even from here.

She moved further along the sand, hoping that Kieron would go, annoyed with herself for this little trick that suddenly seemed like a fit of madness. He followed her though, his eyes never leaving her.

'Is Dan going to bring you to the studios?' he asked with a glance that embarrassed her. 'I could take you out, show you around.'

'I'll be going back to England. I have a career to sort out,' she said briefly.

'Dan's rolling in money, surely he won't let you work? Doesn't he intend to keep you close by?'

'He does not! This guardian business is merely a legal tangle of short duration. I'll have plenty of money of my own soon. I'm here to get well.'

'You look wonderful to me!' He took her arm, and before she could snap at him she found Dan behind them. Neither of them had heard him approach across the soft sand.

'Anita needs you,' he informed Kieron tightly. 'With a bit of luck we'll have this thing all sewn up by tonight, and then you can all be on your way!'

He was hardly the gracious host, and Kieron turned and marched off. Anna looked after him.

'Did you have to be so rude to Kieron?' she asked crossly.

'Yes, I had to be so rude to Kieron,' he mocked. 'Where were you going with him? Did you intend to offer him a few home comforts?'

Anna's reaction was instant. She slapped his face hard and then, seeing the mounting fury, she turned and raced across the sand, heading out along the beach towards the sandy dunes away from the house. He pursued relentlessly, his face grim as she glanced back.

Her nerve broke and she began to run faster, heading inland and making for the house by a circuitous route. He easily outpaced her, especially when she came down on the soft sand, her sarong getting around her ankles

and tripping her neatly. She rolled quickly to get up but Dan was already there, crouching over her, his black shirt open to the waist.

'Panic?' he enquired coldly. 'Do you expect the spanking you deserve for that slap or for this exotic appearance? You wanted to get Amery all hot and bothered?'

'I'm more covered than I was in my bikini!' She was panting after her run and the fall, and she lay there looking up at him defiantly. His many crimes were right at the top of her mind. At this moment she hated Dan and her eyes were blazing, her voice sharp.

'And much more suggestive!' he grated. 'He's white with passion and Anita is a pale shade of green.'

'Serves her right,' Anna raged. 'Maybe now she won't want to stay!'

'You want us to be back to our nice little domestic arrangement?' he asked silkily, and she looked determinedly away from the growing awareness in those tawny eyes.

'I was thinking of Josie,' she muttered uneasily.

She made a move to get up, but he held her shoulders flat to the sand, his gaze running slowly over her, resting on the frantically beating pulse in her neck, the quick rise and fall of her breasts.

'Do you know how you look?' he muttered angrily. 'No wonder Anita went into a panic! You're every man's secret dream, and she knows it. Slender, exotic, slightly wild. You're like that hibiscus, glowing, unreal. A man would want you no matter how he got you!'

He lowered his head, his lips searching her skin softly, moving down her neck to the deep hollow between her breasts.

'Dan!'

Her anxious voice went unnoticed as he came down slowly on top of her, his long length lowered deliberately, stretched out sensuously to cover her and press her into the soft sand.

'Do you think I'm any different?' he asked huskily. 'Are you relying on the past to save you when you let me see you like this? The past is over, Anna! I want you in any way I can get you!'

He lifted his head and looked at her, desire darkening those wonderful eyes, and she was held by the look she saw, by the desire that flared through it. She moved urgently to escape while she could, but her movement only inflamed him further and his hands moved to her breasts, capturing them and moulding them, his eyes never leaving hers. She gasped in wild excitement and fear as he unclipped the black top of her bikini and allowed his eyes to move slowly over the swollen silk of her breasts.

'You beautiful little witch!'

The bronze-gold of his head bent until his lips were brushing the surging, alert peaks, and she shuddered with arousal, a small sound of desire escaping from her parted lips. She made no attempt to resist, and he groaned softly as his mouth covered the painful tightness, his lips closing over the throbbing peak.

She gave in without a struggle, her hands lacing into the thick, gleaming hair, cradling his head as her body arched against his demand. It was almost barbaric. Waves of pleasure surged through her as his tongue probed deeply. Her fingers curled against his shoulders and then slid beneath the opened shirt, clenching on his hot, damp skin, and the pressure of his body increased, every inch of it an unspoken command.

There was no doubt that he had expected her reaction, that he knew she would not resist. His hand slid beneath the parted fabric of the sarong and moved possessively over her leg, coming to rest between her thighs, and she twisted madly, raising her hips to his. The gleaming head lifted and his other hand covered her breast as his eyes moved hotly over her face.

'Tell me what I know perfectly well!' he demanded thickly. 'Tell me what I wait every day to hear.'

His eyes blazed into hers, his teeth gently biting at her lips, his fingers moving on her breast with slow caresses that fired her wild desire. She moaned and twisted against him, the open position on the beach forgotten, her whole world encapsulated in Dan.

'Tell me, Anna,' he murmured against her lips, and she sobbed out the words that had been in her heart for so long.

'I want you, Dan!' Her eyes opened and met his, desire, pain and a look that was almost anger in their dark depths. 'You're mine!'

The sensuous lips smiled slowly, the tawny eyes narrowing with a deep understanding.

'Then kiss me, mermaid,' he ordered thickly. 'Kiss me as if you meant it!'

She looked at those sensuous, tempting lips that waited so possessively, and with a little cry of frustration she raised her head slightly and pressed her own lips hungrily to his. Immediately his mouth covered her own, cutting off any protests, hungrily claiming her as he gathered her against him, no restraint between them at all.

It was madness! They were only just out of sight of the others, but there was always madness when Dan

kissed her. She was molten in his arms, hungry and aching.

'Dan! Dan! Where are you?' Anita's voice came clearly and angrily across the sand. 'Dan, we need you now!'

He lifted his head and gazed down at Anna's face. She was too bemused to feel any confusion yet and he knew it. He fastened the clasp of her bikini, his touch gentle and unhurried, then he slowly stood, pulling her to her feet.

'Dan! Where the devil are you?'

Closer than ever, Anita's voice at last penetrated Anna's dazed mind, and with it came realisation of her own words and actions; but the shame she should have felt never came. She had given in to her lifelong love for Dan and he knew it. His face was filled with a kind of exultation as he gently turned her towards the house, her route hidden by trees, and she went blindly, her whole being like a floating cloud, softened, vulnerable and overwhelmed.

The evening started quite well, everyone managing to behave in a civilised way, but, in spite of Dan's terse manner on the beach when he had almost ordered Kieron back to the house, Anna found herself almost under seige. Kieron followed her wherever she went, and there was little she could do about it without actually turning on him.

Fortunately Dan was not annoyed with her; his furious looks seemed to be divided between Kieron and Anita, the latter actually annoying Dan more. She flatly refused to work on after dinner, and as they had been here for two days it looked as if they would be here longer.

'Let's take the whole damned thing and get back to the studio with it!' Anita said petulantly. 'I work better there. It's time you came back to California, Dan, in any case. Anna could come with you, you don't have to hang around here. You'll still be together in California. You've got an apartment there.'

It was a snide remark and Dan instantly bridled.

'I'm not *hanging around* here,' he rasped. 'I *live* here! Anna does not have to be under my wing either. She's an adult, not a child!'

'Well, darling, if that's your attitude, then it looks as if we're here for another day—or two,' Anita murmured.

Anna expected an explosion from Dan, but he surprised her.

'Can't be helped,' he said blithely. 'It's a bit rough, though, all this hard work. Tomorrow morning we'll have a break. We'll go diving. It's time Anna had another lesson. How about it?' He looked across at Dean Orton, who grinned and nodded.

'I'm game, any time. How about you, Kieron?'

'A break will do us all good. Anna must be bored with all this script-writing and alterations. I'll show her a few tricks.'

Dan's lips quirked, but he made no comment, and Anna felt a wave of irritation mixed with dismay. He was so sure of her that he wasn't even annoyed with Kieron any more. She supposed that everyone fell into his arms. He was just preparing to add her to the number.

'You know I hate things like diving!' Anita said angrily. 'I've told you before.'

'You're not obliged to go,' Dan assured her pleasantly. 'You can stay and go over the script, or just laze about.

We have to have a break, though, and we're certainly going.'

'I'll stay here!' Anita snapped, and Kieron's face was only just controlled. It was easy to read his mind; he intended to make a nuisance of himself without the cold eyes of Anita on him. Anna expected Anita to order him to stay, but she didn't. He became emboldened.

'I'll give you a hand with your diving, Anna,' he offered with a knowing look at her that infuriated her.

'Why, thank you very much!'

She waited for Dan to intervene, but he didn't, and as they all began to talk again, Dean and Kieron trying to placate Anita without looking as if they were doing it, Anna walked out on to the veranda, her angry eyes staring out to sea.

Her own reaction frustrated her. She had wanted him to be possessive in there, wanted him to show it, and she knew he could not. This was a secret, a dark secret, and she knew that well enough.

What right had she to be so angry anyway? She was merely a passing interest to Dan, and only because she had thrown herself at him. He had a son! Her mind told her that over and over, but the thought didn't bring with it the shame that it should have done, and she was swept with a feeling of self-disgust. Dan was probably just enjoying a boost to his male ego. Her heart begged it to be more than that, but she was not a fool.

She heard a quiet step behind her and she knew it was Dan without even looking round; her whole being instantly recognised him, it always had done.

'Not sleepy?' He came to stand behind her, and she took a deep, steadying breath.

'Not at the moment.'

'Want to walk on the beach?' His hand slid over her arm and she pulled her arm away angrily, more annoyed with herself for the feelings that shot through her than with him.

'Ah! You're in one of those tempers. You've been thinking. I might have known that clever little mind would go into overdrive!'

He was laughing at her, although his voice was perfectly serious, and she realised what a fool he must think her, her actions earlier on the beach now embarrassing her.

'I'm not in a temper,' she said smoothly. 'What makes you think that? I'm really looking forward to the diving tomorrow. It will be exciting to have a whole group of people there.'

'Oh, very!' he murmured. 'Just imagine, Anita left behind and three men all to yourself.'

'Don't be so damned sarcastic!' She tried to move away, but his arms came down on either side of the rail, trapping her.

'Make a list of the things I'm allowed to be and I'll try to oblige,' he murmured against her hair. 'You know I'd do anything for you.'

'And don't be patronising with me! I can well do without being treated like an irritated child.'

He swung her round, his hands tight on her waist, his thumbs softly probing against her hips.

'They'll be gone soon, sweetheart,' he reminded her softly. 'As soon as I can get rid of them I will. I want you to myself.'

'Don't bother! I'm beginning to get used to them.' She looked up at him coolly, annoyed that he had called her 'sweetheart' and not meant it. How many other

words like that did he use to women? Jealousy tore into her and she added, 'Anyway, Kieron is going to teach me a few tricks!'

His hands tightened painfully.

'If he comes within ten yards of you, I'll teach him a neat trick—I'll drown him! You're mine!'

'You've no right to say that.' Her heart took off at an alarming rate as her legs weakened.

'Why not? This afternoon on the beach you looked up into my eyes and said the same thing. What's good for the goose...'

She could see his eyes gleaming at her and she looked away rapidly.

'I was scared and then—then agitated. I went a little mad, I think!'

'Don't worry, it's a state that can easily be produced again when they've gone.'

'I intend to leave with them.'

His face was no longer mocking. His arm came tightly around her and his hand tilted her face cruelly.

'Words come cheap! It's deeds that count! You're going nowhere at all!'

'For how long?' She struggled but it was useless, for his grip merely tightened. 'You can't just keep me here.'

'Well,' he said quietly, 'you could appeal to Kieron to rescue you. He looks just about ready to howl with frustration!'

'You think you can say just anything to me, don't you?' There were tears at the back of her voice and he heard them, but it did not lessen his temper.

'No, I don't, although you deserve it! I know all about frustration. I'm ready to howl myself, and the moon reminds me!'

He lowered his head and his lips covered hers harshly, pressing with punishing force against her own, and she realised that it was not possible to provoke a man like Dan Toren and get away with it. He had taken her into his life to look after her when she needed help, he had cared for her and been kind.

It was all her own fault that this was happening. Her childhood fixation with Dan had grown into something that was now controlling her actions, and all shame had left her. She was even glorying in this angry treatment. It was Dan who would be ashamed of himself.

He was! He let her go abruptly and turned to walk into the house, and her hand went out to him, although he didn't see it.

'Dan, I'm sorry!'

He didn't even answer, and when she went inside he was already in his room, the door tightly closed. Even the door seemed angry.

There was no getting out of the trip next day. No matter how annoyed Dan was, he had said that there would be diving and he meant it. She was back to being a nuisance, his whole demeanour told her that. He took her cylinder to the launch and then handed her everything else, bundling the things into her arms. He was not about to wait on her hand and foot this time.

She had a T-shirt on over her bikini but it did not put Kieron off at all; his eyes strayed over her slender, brown legs, but this morning Dan didn't even notice—or, if he *did* notice, he didn't care. If she hadn't hurried he would have set off without her, and she avoided his gaze all the time. It was so angry that it almost burned her.

As Dan slowed the launch and came to a stop within the quiet waters of the little bay, Anna felt a wave of sadness. The last time she had been here with Dan, things had been different. He had not known how she felt, he had only suspected. Now he knew, and the companionship they had carefully built, the companionship she had wanted all her life, was gone.

What did he feel? With painful clarity his words of nearly five years ago rang in her ears. 'Respond to any man like that and you'll get kissed like that!' She was supposed to be clever, but she didn't learn very well, not when it was Dan. She expected too much of him, wanted her idol back; it was all dreaming.

She never once asked for help. She got herself into her wetsuit, only aware that Dan was checking on her when she looked up after zipping herself carefully in it to find his eyes on her activities. Kieron picked up her air cylinder, but Dan simply took it out of his hands and came across to fix it for her. Still, he refused to speak to her at all.

All she could do was follow last time's instructions, and as they all fell neatly into the clear water she made her careful descent, more scared than she had been the last time. She felt on her own and quite incapable of managing.

She dipped her mask and let herself float away, only then looking down to find Dan hovering gracefully in the water beneath her, his eyes on her movements. When he signalled sharply to her, she followed.

In spite of her gloomy thoughts, the underwater world soon held her entranced, and this time she lingered, following Dan more slowly, going deeper to look more closely at the coral, hovering enchanted as the small,

brilliantly coloured fish brushed against her and looked at her with staring, round eyes that seemed to hold their own inquisitiveness.

The world above was forgotten, and she longed to touch the beautiful coral that looked like flowers of pink and white. Dan's words, though, stuck in her mind, and she was no more inclined to disobey him than she had been as a child. Kieron left her well alone; in fact, she couldn't even see him, and she realised that he would have to be pretty thick-skinned not have got the point as Dan had firmly taken the air cylinder from him and seen to her himself.

She was glad. She tried a few tricks in the water herself, twisting and turning as she had seen Dan do, coming to an irritated halt as she felt one of her flippers slowly easing itself off. She had been so determined to see to herself that she had hurried and probably not put it on correctly. As she was reaching for it, it came off and floated downwards, out of her reach.

She felt surprisingly naked without it and she went down to get it. It was only then that she realised how deep the water was. It had lodged itself in coral, and she felt that she had been going down for a long time before her searching hand carefully retrieved it.

There was almost a feeling of panic to get back to the surface, and she kicked out to rise, wincing with the sudden pain as her foot struck against coral that felt like hard rock and not at all the delicate thing it seemed to be. It wasn't the first time she had cut her foot on coral since she had been here; she had done it on the beach, but this time it hurt badly. Dan would be annoyed at her carelessness. She looked round quickly but he was

not there, and she was at the surface before he appeared, swimming back to find her.

It was hard pulling herself to the deck, and she found that Dean was already there.

'Had enough?' He grinned at her and helped her over the last few feet.

'I think so. Dan said we weren't staying more than an hour, didn't he?'

'Yes. The script has to be thrashed out. If we stay here longer, then Dan's going to thrash Anita, I think, and I'm probably going to line up for my turn at her!' He laughed across at her as she peeled off her suit. 'Anyway, girlie, time's money!'

Dan came on deck as they were laughing, and he didn't look very amused. She was pulling off the trousers over her feet, and as she stood a sharp pain jabbed through her foot, making her wince.'

'What's the matter?'

Dan was standing aggressively over her at once, and she wasn't about to tell him that she had lost her flipper through careless preparation and then kicked her foot against hard coral because she was in a panic to get to the surface.

'Nothing. A stitch, I think. I did a few fancy twirls down there.'

'So I noticed. All without tuition!' He turned as Kieron came over the side. 'Ah! Here's the man with the tricks!'

'Never mind the tricks,' Dean said in a low voice, his words lost to Kieron. 'What the hell are we going to do about Anita?'

'Work her to death, as murder is punishable by law!' Dan said sardonically. 'The time is fast approaching

when I'll refuse to alter another thing. I wouldn't be altering now if it hadn't been for...'

'I know.' Dean patted Dan's arm, and Anna wondered what on earth they were talking about, but they both dropped quiet as Kieron came across, and Dan looked at him fairly pleasantly.

'Let's get back to Anita,' he suggested. 'The sooner we get down to it, the sooner you'll be able to leave!'

'Tempt me with sugar, not medicine!' Kieron muttered, his eyes on Anna. 'Who the hell wants to leave?'

'I do!' Dean snapped. 'This film has a limited budget. If Anita hangs around complaining much longer we'll be running pretty close to the line.'

Anna was only half listening. She was longing to lift her foot up and see what it was that was hurting so much, but not while Dan was there. Every time she twisted her foot around his eyes flashed to her, and she felt like someone playing hide and seek. It could wait until they got back.

Even in the privacy of her room she could see nothing at all. There was a small black mark where she had hit the coral; the beginning of a bruise, she supposed. But, in spite of the hard bang, the coral hadn't cut her at all, not that she could see. It was painful to stand on, though, and she made a small pad of cotton wool and managed fairly well, her sandals hiding this rough dressing. If Dan had been at all sympathetic towards her she would have told him, but he was as hard as he had been all day and she tried to fade into the background, a skill she had acquired early in life as far as Dan was concerned.

A miserable evening followed a miserable afternoon. Dan was at the end of his patience with Anita, and the

air was so thick with displeasure that Kieron did his own fading into the background.

'If we're not finished tonight, I'll have to think of some excuse to flee!' he muttered to Anna after dinner, when Dean and Anita trailed behind Dan to his study. 'She's doing this on purpose.'

'Whatever for?'

Anna couldn't understand anyone like Anita, and she wondered how the woman ever got anything done.

'You're really a sweet young thing, aren't you?' Kieron said drily. 'Nita was expecting to have Dan all to herself. What did she find but an exotic little companion who's not allowed to stray more than a few feet from Dan.'

'It's a small island!' Anna got out irritably, her face flushing.

'He makes it smaller when you're there.'

'I believe you've been told all about Dan and I!' she snapped jumping up and regretting it at once as her foot seemed to catch fire.

Dan came in at that moment, and at the sight of her agitation and her flushed face he strode over and almost ordered Kieron out into the study.

'Keep away from him!' he snapped as Anna stood there, biting her lips with pain.

'Chance would be a fine thing!' she said almost tearfully. 'Just leave me alone!'

He looked at her narrow-eyed. 'That's hardly likely, is it?' he jeered softly. His face suddenly looked less angry.

'Is something hurting you?'

'No!' she assured him quickly. 'I'm just thoroughly fed up with this constant battling. I want to leave when they do!'

Instead of anger there was amusement on his face, and he walked forward to hold her shoulders firmly.

'Do you say that merely to hear me tell you that I won't allow it?' he asked softly, his smile widening when she shook her head vigorously. 'You don't want to go, I don't want you to go, so let's not even talk about it. You were captured long before I knew exactly how you felt.'

'I don't feel...'

He lowered his gleaming head and kissed her swiftly, his hands twisted in her hair.'

'Stop it, baby!' he said roughly, turning to walk out as she raised dazed eyes and saw Anita just disappearing into the hall.

Any suspicions she had about them were now confirmed, Anna thought fatefully. It was all one great big muddle that would only get worse. She wandered off to bed, a little frightened when she imagined that the dark mark under her foot seemed to be swollen. It was only to be expected, she told herself firmly. It had been quite a bang. She cheered herself up by reminding herself that it could have been her nose. Nevertheless, it hurt.

She was just about to get into bed when a sharp knock on the door had her stopping and getting back into her dressing-gown.

'Come in!' She hoped it wasn't Kieron on any amorous excursion, and it wasn't, but her face was no less astounded when it turned out to be Anita.

'Did you want something?' She wasn't going to pretend any friendliness, not after the way Anita had behaved and after the things she had heard her say that night on the veranda.

'I just wanted to warn you about the danger you're placing yourself in,' Anita said quietly, her red-painted fingernails like claws on the door. 'I had my suspicions, but now I know why you're here. Don't think you're the first. Dan has a succession of women, but there's only one that he cares about. I don't suppose you know about Daphne?'

'All about her!' Anna said angrily. 'I've met her and even spent a week in her company, and this is none of your business!'

'If you think Dan will give her up, then you're mistaken,' Anita assured her. 'They've been together for over four years and it's as permanent as Dan is ever likely to get!'

'I don't need any advice from you. If you think there's anything that shouldn't be happening here, then point it out to Dan. In the meantime, you're a guest in his house. I wonder how he'd react if he suddenly walked in now?'

It made Anita a little worried, Anna could tell that, and she drove the point home.

'Dan is already furious about this delay in things. If you're not ready to leave soon with the script satisfactory, he's going to refuse to alter anything!'

'He wouldn't dare!' There was just the touch of fear at the back of the spiteful eyes.

'He would! He doesn't need any more money. Dean Orton is also annoyed. Maybe there'll be a new star in this film if you don't buck up, especially if I tell Dan about this little chat!'

It worked and Anita left very quickly. Anna was shaking. She didn't need to be told about Dan's lifestyle, she had already found out about that. It hurt too

badly to have it pushed at her again. The foot was throbbing and she took off her dressing-gown, preparing to slide into bed and hope for sleep.

Dan just walked in without so much as a tap on the door.

'Did I see Anita leave this room?' he asked aggressively.

'You did!' She was beginning to get annoyed as well as pained. This was like a railway station; soon the others would burst in.

'What did she want?'

'She wanted to borrow a cup of poison, but unfortunately I don't have any brewed at the moment!' Anna snapped. 'Maybe tomorrow!'

'Anna!' He moved forward threateningly and she dived into bed, hurting her foot even more.

'Oh, get out!' she sobbed, sliding under the sheets and turning her back.

'Anna.' His voice softened, but she lay as stiff as a rod, her face hidden.

'Just go, Dan. I don't want you here, in fact I don't want you anywhere!' To her relief it annoyed him, and the next sound she heard was her door banging as he left.

CHAPTER EIGHT

IN THE morning Anna felt very ill; her foot was throbbing and, when she looked, the instep was so swollen that it filled the space between her toes and heel with no curve whatever. She had to tell Dan. Getting out of bed took all her courage and it was impossible to put her foot to the ground. She felt feverish, light-headed, her whole world one of pain.

She was just at the door when she heard the launch leave, and she stumbled along the passage in time to see it swing out into the wide turquoise waters and head for Nassau. Incredibly they had gone. Her words of the previous night must have had some effect, but Dan was gone too, taking them to Nassau.

'Dan!' Foolishly she shouted, although she knew he was far out of range of any voice, and her rather desperate cry brought Josie hurrying from the kitchen.

'Mr Dan, he's gone to take them away!' she said in a gleeful voice and then her eyes fell properly on Anna. 'Oh, my dear lord!'

Anna heard her calling frantically for Abe and then she fainted.

The only memories she had were of pain. She came round once to see Abe standing in the smaller launch, his lanky figure leaning forward as if to drive it on faster, and she found that her head was cradled in Josie's ample lap.

'You goin' to be all right. Abe is goin' to catch Mr Dan at the quay and he's goin' to have you in hospital so fast you won't even know it!'

There was blackness again and confusion. At one time she felt strong arms reach for her and she knew it was Dan. She was so sure that she murmured his name, but he didn't answer and she knew he was angry with her for this further trouble. She tried to explain but he wouldn't let her, he just pulled her face to his shoulder and held her too tightly.

It was all over, she knew that. She had caused so much turmoil in his tranquil life, kept him from California and Daphne, kept him from his son. She would never go back to Amara Cay. Distantly she heard herself telling him, her own words ringing in her mind. 'I'll never go back to the island, never, never!'

She awoke to a bright, sunny room, a comfortable, white bed, and at first she couldn't take it in. She moved her foot gingerly but it wasn't painful, just a little tender. How had they done it so quickly, and where was Dan?

'Hello! Awake and alert at last. We were beginning to wonder when it would happen!'

It was a doctor, and he walked to the bed to smile down at her.

'I don't seem to know where I am.'

She smiled up at him rather tentatively, the anxiety in her at the thought of Dan keeping her silent when she wanted to ask about him. She seemed to have a vague memory of Dan being there, in fact she could almost feel him in the room, but she dreaded bringing up the subject.

'You're in Nassau, in hospital.' He looked at her seriously. 'You're a very lucky young lady. If it hadn't been for Mr Toren's servants' quick action and Mr Toren's own speed in getting you here, I shudder to think what the consequences would have been.'

'My—my foot was so painful. Did you look at it? It doesn't hurt much now.'

'I looked at it and operated on it, and no, it won't hurt much now. You've been here for a week. It's had time to heal.'

'A week?' Dim memories flooded back, memories of Dan, talking to him, explaining. 'Was Mr Toren here?'

'All the time. He left last night for the first time when the fever broke and you went into a sound sleep. I doubt if he's slept for the whole week more than the odd few minutes. He refused to leave. I suppose he's in some way responsible for your well-being?' There was this look again. The same speculating look that seemed to come her way so often when Dan was mentioned, and she longed to either lie or tell him to mind his own business. 'I sent him to get some sleep,' he continued when it became apparent that she was not about to enlighten him, 'but I've little doubt that he'll be back later.'

'What—why did my foot...?'

'Coral. A small piece was lodged under the skin. That type of coral can cause a fever if you just get a sharp jab from it. You did better than that. You got a fair-sized piece in your foot and kept it there. It had a field day! Mr Toren, of course, explained about the diving, but he said you had flippers on.'

'Not all the time.' She explained about her minor accident and he looked more severe than ever, every last

bit of speculation leaving his eyes and a hard, reprimanding look taking over.

'It should have been attended to at once. Even then, you would have needed medical treatment. I can't understand why you told nobody!'

Pride, she thought. Pride and shame and a desire to escape from Dan's censure. She could no more stand that from him now than she ever could, and it had caused all this trouble. What would he think now? She closed her eyes before she disgraced herself completely by crying, and the doctor left the room silently.

Dan came later and she was shocked at the sight of his pale face, the tired look in his eyes.

'How do you feel?' He sat by the bed but made no attempt to touch her. 'They say you can leave in a couple of days, but you know best how you feel.'

'I feel a bit weak, but apart from that I'm perfectly fine.'

'All right. I'll make arrangements for you to leave in two days, then.'

'Will—will you fetch me?'

She was suddenly desperately anxious. He was quite cold, distant, and she felt that terrible wave of loneliness again.

'No. I have to leave tonight for the States. The script wasn't finished, but Anita demanded to go. It has to be finished now. There's money hanging on the time factor.'

'I—I know. Dean told me. How will I get back to the island? Will Abe fetch me?'

'No. You're not going back to Amara Cay! You're going home. I'll have all your things brought here before I leave for America, and I'll have you a ticket to London waiting at the airport. I've already had money trans-

ferred to your bank. It will be ready for you when you get home.'

'You said I couldn't leave,' she reminded him in dismay. 'You said you wouldn't let me go!'

'An amorous game, Anna! I have things to do, commitments of my own, so do you. You go home as soon as you leave hospital!' His voice was harsh and cold, and the tawny eyes never flinched when she looked at him.

'I have no home.' Her dark eyes seemed to fill her face and he moved irritably, a frown creasing his tanned brow.

'You have plenty of money and a first-class honours degree. You have a life in England and I have one here. You never wanted a guardian, and heaven knows I never wanted the job anyway! I can remember when you were determined to go overseas. I can also remember that you had a career planned in any number of spheres! As to a home, you're almost twenty-two and there's Langford Hall.'

'No, there isn't, not any more.'

She slid down the bed, turning her face away into the pillow. He didn't want her. He never had, except for those few times when she had thrown all self-respect away and almost begged to be loved. He was stepping back into his own life, back to Daphne, back to a little boy called Trevor. The island days were over. Dan had never belonged to her.

She heard her own pained cry on the beach. 'You're mine!' He had said it too, but he hadn't meant it. An amorous game, a game he was used to. She closed her eyes and shut the tears inside, and he stood for a moment before walking out.

'Goodbye, Anna.' His hand touched her hair and then he was gone.

Tears never came, they would not. She asked herself what she had expected. It was no shock, really. She had always know that Dan belonged to someone else, she had known that for nearly five years. It was just that she was obsessed with him, thoughts of him filling every waking moment and most of her dreams. She would have been anything he wanted her to be. He didn't want her to be anything. He just wanted her out of his life, as he had always done.

She had never expected to have another visitor, but on her last day in hospital Josie came, her dark face round and anxious until she saw that Anna was well again. She was resplendent in her visiting clothes, her white hat sitting proudly on her head.

'You give us some shock,' she said earnestly. 'Abe and me, we thought you was a goner!'

'I'm really stupid,' Anna admitted, touched by Josie's concern. 'I made so much trouble.'

'I'm sure goin' to miss you, honey,' Josie confessed almost tearfully. 'I had to get here early before I go over to the island for the day. We'll be late but I wanted to see you before you go home to England. We brought your cases in last night,' she added mournfully.

'Yes. I'll have to be getting up soon ready for the flight. I'm glad you came, Josie. I'm going to miss you, too. There's not going to be much to do at the island now that Mr Toren is in California, though. It doesn't matter if you're late, does it?'

'He ain't in California, honey!' Josie assured her, giving her an anxious look, no doubt wondering if she

was still feverish. 'He's right there on Amara, as tight
as a drum and as mad as hell! That there film star upset
everything. Mr Dan's going to be days recovering, then
he was here all that week with you, not sleeping. It's not
the same now. I sure wish you were coming back!'

Anna heard nothing but the one piece of information
that shook her. Dan was not in America. He had lied
to her. He had wanted her out of his life so much that
he had been prepared to lie. It told her more than any
words could tell. She was glad when Josie looked
worriedly at the clock and said she would have to go.
She had never felt so unwanted, so shunned. The time
for her plane could not come soon enough.

Everything had been laid on to make her departure
smooth. A taxi collected her, her ticket was waiting for
her and all she had to do was keep on walking. Her foot
was little more than a minor irritation now, and she had
been given strict instructions about keeping an eye on
it. At the last minute the doctor had looked a little surprised that she was simply going back to England, but
she had kept her own counsel. She always would.

The other passengers barged into her, tourists going
home. That was where she was going, home! She stared
straight ahead and just nodded vaguely at the taxi driver
when he put her bags down; even his tip had been dealt
with. Dan was ruthlessly efficient. She was left standing
with her luggage, lost in an island of grief as the other
people washed around her with a kind of frantic energy.

She was pushed aside frequently, never seeming to get
to the counter to check in her baggage, and finally she
pulled it out of the way, sitting down to stare at it for
no good reason. There seemed to be a panicky feeling
here, but it hardly touched her. She felt as if she was

held by a strong, tight thread that wouldn't let go, the plane a monstrous thing that would take her from Dan.

Her thoughts turned homewards and were lost in dismay. The rest of her life without him was a black and horrifying thought. The thread pulled tighter and held her fast as she realised that whatever had been in her life before was now gone. Elaine and Steve, Bryan, her days at Oxford were mere dreams, hardly touching her. There was only Dan, and panic welled up in her throat at the thought of leaving him. She was prepared to beg for a little more time. One more time to see his face. One more time to watch him walk towards her. It was little to ask. She would go back to England tomorrow. She could pay her own fare.

'I don't want to go on this plane. Can I hand the ticket in for someone else?' The woman at the desk looked at her as if she was out of her mind, but she shrugged and nodded.

'Leave your name and address and you can have a refund. We have more passengers than places. There'll be no difficulty in filling one seat. Somebody's going to bless you!'

But not Dan. He would be coldly angry. It didn't matter, what mattered was seeing him this last time, filling her memory with him to sustain her through the future. She left her bags at the left luggage and hurried out to get a taxi to the quay, not at all sure as to how to proceed from there, but filled with a great burst of nervous energy.

There were a few boats in and a few men standing around talking. It was unnaturally still, hot and dry, and they all ignored her.

'Can I get a boat out to Amara Cay? It's terribly urgent!'

She was in a white dress, a small case in her hand with enough clothes for one day. After that, Dan would throw her out, probably frog-march her up the steps of the next plane, but for now she could see nothing but his face.

The men seemed to be holding a wordless discussion, their eyes going from the sea and sky to her anxious face and back again. It was her anxiety that won, she was sure.

'I'll take her. My boat's faster than either of yours.'

The man was reluctant and got her into the boat with speed, but she was not looking for gallantry, she just wanted to see Dan. The man was silent and the boat simply flew, pushed to the limit, she was certain. She knew that these people were not at all talkative until they knew you, and that then they never stopped talking. This man was no exception, but he made no attempt to introduce any conversation, and even if he had she would have been too agitated to reply. His sole concern was speed, though, and as he came carefully to the small quay at Amara he leapt out and lifted her to the wooden landing before she had any chance to make a move.

'How much do I...?'

Her case was beside her and he was already in gear and moving out.

'Mr Toren pays, next time you in Nassau!' He just shouted out to her, already moving into the next gear. She wondered what was going on in Nassau. He wasn't even interested in money. No wonder he hadn't been interested in her! He was out, turned and away before she even had her small case in her hand, and she felt

quite glad. If Dan had seen her arrive, he would have paid gladly to put her back on board.

It dawned on her then that Dan's launch wasn't here; neither was Abe's. The whole place was silent, the calm of the sea, the stillness of the air and the utter silence of the island uncanny. She began to walk to the house, looking at it as she had once looked at Langford Hall, seeing it afresh with eyes that knew it was for the last time. The gardens looked so bright, the lawns so green, the hibiscus by the veranda brilliantly glowing. It reminded her of the one she had placed in her hair, of her words to Dan on the beach, the distressed cry that had come from her heart.

He was not here. How could he be? If he had been here, he would have heard the boat come in. She walked into the house, her own footsteps the only sound, and then she began to go from room to room. The house was deserted, and so, apparently, was the island. She stood in the hall for a second, irresolute, unable to understand it all. Had Dan gone to California after all? Had Josie been mistaken? Perhaps she had arrived to find that Dan was preparing to leave and had then gone back to Nassau with Abe.

A strong breeze began to blow from the sea and Anna welcomed the suddenly cooler air, the end of the unnatural stillness. It was blowing sand into the hall, a thing that had never happened before, and almost absentmindedly she walked across to shut the door, her eyes not really seeing anything, her mind too puzzled. What was she going to do now? She sat down on the edge of a chair, trying to think it all out, jumping alarmingly as the front door opened and then banged shut.

As she hurried into the hall, her heart leapt to see Dan dusting sand from his clothes, his thick hair untidy and windswept. At first he didn't see her, but she took one hesitant step forward and he looked up in surprise, his eyes widening in shock as he saw who was there.

'Anna!'

He was like someone carved from stone and her nerve deserted her entirely. Words refused to come. She could neither move nor look away.

'What the hell are you doing here?' His face was furious and he took one menacing step towards her. 'Why aren't you on that plane?'

'I—I let it go. I wanted to...'

He strode across and grasped her shoulders, shaking her, his eyes blazing down at her, anger in every fibre of his body.

'What did you want? Answer me! I told you that you weren't coming back here. I don't want you here! Why have you come back?'

His hands were hurting, biting into her shoulders, and her head fell before the force of his furious rejection. 'I wanted to see you. I wanted to... just once more...'

It was only a whisper, there were too many tears choking her, and his whole body went still. Slowly he released her shoulders, and she thought he was going to walk away and leave her standing there. She had been prepared to beg, and it seemed that she would have to. But he gave a strange, deep sigh and pulled her into his arms, holding her tightly, his face against her hair.

'You crazy little thing!' he said harshly. 'Why did you have to come back? Why now?'

'Let me stay tonight, Dan,' she pleaded, unable to raise her head, his arms holding her too tightly. 'Tomorrow I'll go and never come back!'

'Maybe you'll get more than you bargained for,' he warned in a gruff voice, his hand tilting her face. He shook his head ruefully, his lips twisted wryly. 'There's no alternative but to stay now, whether I want you to or not. I've got the launch anchored out at the other side of the island, everything lashed down as tightly as I can. That's where I was when you came, obviously. There's no other way of leaving Amara Cay. By the time I got the boat back round here and you into it, it would be too late!'

'Too late?' He was so deadly serious, and she looked at him urgently.

'You've come back to face a hurricane, Anna!' His eyes ran over her strained face, the long black hair and her slender neck. 'Now we'll find out just what sort of mermaid you are! Let's hope that Neptune realises you're here and remembers that you're one of his own.'

He let her go and stood away, glancing at his watch.

'We've got about two hours, if that. Let's move!'

She didn't much care what she was facing so long as Dan was there, and as he strode into the kitchen she almost ran behind him.

'As you're here, you may as well make yourself useful. Don't count on two hours, either. At the moment we've got power. Make a meal, make sandwiches for later, find any vacuum flasks we have and fill them with hot drinks.' He turned and gripped her arms. 'And from now until this is over, when I tell you to do something you do it at once! Is that clear?'

There was no sign of the rueful humour and she nodded quickly, his urgent words reaching her even through her feeling of elation that he had clasped her so tightly to him, although it had been preceded by a shaking.

'Whatever you say!'

He glanced at her ironically and walked out, and she soon heard banging coming from the back of the house; but she got on resolutely with her own tasks. There were plenty of them. She had no idea what a hurricane was, other than the stormy scenes she had seen on films. It would have been exciting, but right now the excitement of being near Dan was uppermost, and his attitude to the coming storm had been too serious for her to take it lightly. She hurried with everything, only taking off a few minutes to slip to her room and change into the jeans and shirt she had brought with her.

She finished her other tasks while the meal was cooking and went into the hall as Dan came striding back, grim-faced.

'It's ready.'

'Keep it hot, we can't take time to eat now—and get some sort of woolly with you,' he added, his eyes skimming over her.

'I haven't got one. My luggage is in Nassau.' Her voice faltered as his eyes glanced at her accusingly. She shouldn't even be here. It was all in the one sharp look.

'Get one of mine. You'll have to get it yourself and leave it where you can lay hands on it. It may well turn cold. I've really no idea.'

'Can—can I go in your room and...'

He simply glared at her. 'Yes, you can go in my room and...'

He strode out and she bit her lip. Everything she said made matters worse. She hurried to Dan's room and looked quickly for a sweater, taking the first one to hand and hurrying out as if chased by devils.

One glance in the kitchen assured her that everything was all right, the meal keeping hot, and then she went to find him. What the banging had been was now clear. He was putting shutters up to all the windows, and he had just reached the front of the house. The wind was picking up quite alarmingly, and when she looked across to the sea her face stiffened in surprise.

It was boiling. The clear turquoise sea was no more. Out towards the east the sea seemed to be piling up, rolling, threatening and unspeakably alive. Breakers crashed on the once tranquil shore and it alarmed her. She was actually looking at a scene she had never looked at before, as if this was a strange place, another island. The beautiful palms were bending almost to the ground, great palm fronds already tossed to the sand. Every plant in the well-cared-for garden would be ruined. There would be no more hibiscus to place in her hair.

'For God's sake, get inside, Anna!' Dan looked across at her angrily and bore down on her, taking her arm and hustling her inside. 'I've got two more shutters to do and then we're battened in. I can't walk around worrying where you've trailed off to. Stay here!'

He pushed her inside and slammed the door which in any case almost blew out of his hands; his urgency took hold of her. He had given her things to do and she had done them. What now?

Pictures she had seen came to her mind and she hurried into the kitchen, taking down glasses, crockery and pans, stowing them away in cupboards, certain that Dan would

ask if she had gone mad, but his furious speed and the desperation of his efforts to finish the tasks was taking hold of her too.

He didn't think she was mad. He came silently in during her hurried packing, and as she looked up he nodded.

'Good girl! A few glasses aren't the real worry, though. Now that we're battened down you can help with something more precious. Get the ornaments and pictures. They have a very special value for me. I had a very good reason for collecting them. I'm damned well not going to see them all shattered.'

He had boxes all ready and they filled them up, neither saying anything about the wind that now seemed to be funnelling round the house. The sea was roaring in a way she had never heard before, the crash of the breakers on the shore alarming. It came to her mind that this was a small island with little high land. The wind and sea had a fury that made the land seem puny and transient. In her mind she could see the waves piled up high, the sea approaching in a great invading mass.

'Is it here now, the hurricane?'

She couldn't keep the anxiety from her voice and he smiled grimly.

'Not yet, really. This might be called the advance guard. The rest comes later.'

They both looked up as thunder shook the house, and Dan stood.

'That's it! We've done well. Now we retreat!'

She had always thought the room at the centre of the house strange; there was something oddly different about

it. Dan dragged the boxes in there and ordered her to stay put.

'The meal!'

'My God, you're an irritating female! Come on!'

They brought everything else in together and, as Anna spread a cloth on a small table and set out the meal, Dan brought in the packs of sandwiches and the flasks and shut the door.

'Eat while you've still got the nerve,' he ordered grimly. 'It may be the last warm meal you get for some time.'

'How long will it last?'

'It's not really here yet.' He shrugged. 'Who knows? Depends how fast it's travelling, where the "eye" is, where it's going.'

They ate in silence. At least, *they* were silent. The noise around the house was growing, frightening gusts adding to the steady, screaming force of the wind, rain now driving against the roof like something desperately trying to enter. Anna pushed her plate away before too long, unable to simply go on eating, moving the table aside as Dan followed suit and put down his knife and fork.

She curled up in a chair, her eyes on his as he sank tiredly to the one settee.

'Scared?' He suddenly looked up at her and she shook her head.

'No. You couldn't say I was scared. Terrified—now you might say that! I can't think at the moment of a bigger word.'

He grinned across at her.

'Come and sit by me. We'll face it together.'

She needed no second invitation. Whatever was happening, she could face it with Dan. She curled up at the

other end of the settee, her eyes on him as he sat with his head back, his whole demeanour weary.

There was a terrible crash and she shot bolt upright, her eyes wide open. Dan reached across, gathering her with his arms and pulling her close.

'What was that?' She felt like burying her head against him, and he must have known because his hand came to her hair, soothing and stroking.

'I would imagine that it was a tree.'

'Is there any chance of one crashing on the house?'

'Unlikely. Although if the hurricane really hits us, then anything might happen.'

'I somehow thought it *had* hit us!' Anna said with shaky humour, but he shook his head.

'If we get a direct hit, we'll be in no doubt. I've seen that happen once.' He leaned back, pulling her with him. 'There's not really any problem at the moment. This is the second house that I've had on Amara Cay, and I took great care that this one would stand anything but a direct hit by a hurricane. It may stand even that—at least, this room should.'

'What happened to the other house?'

'I bought the island and there was already a house here,' he told her. 'Fortunately I was away when the storm came. When I came back there was just devastation. The house was just so much rubble, everything gone. When I had this one built, it was with the first one in mind. The frame is steel reinforced. There isn't a tree close enough to fall on it, and I made this room into a survival room. It's not a beautiful room, but it's sound.'

She looked round. There were candles, water and a substantial first-aid kit, as well as the flasks, and in the corner, on a table, a two-way radio.

As she was looking at it, it came to life.

'Amara Cay! Amara Cay! Can you hear me? Over.'

Dan lifted her aside and went over, taking the microphone and speaking quickly. 'Amara Cay. Go ahead, Johnny! What's the situation? Over.'

'It's not too bad, but there's a great build-up to the east. You're the last island I have to contact. Good luck, Dan!'

There was a fierce crackling and the voice ended abruptly; Dan walked back and sank down beside Anna.

'Here it comes,' he said quietly. 'Why aren't you on that plane and miles from here?'

'I'd rather be here,' she confessed softly. 'Whatever happens, I'd rather be here.'

He pulled her closer and she snuggled against him, closing her eyes as the wind set up a banshee wail that frightened her more than anything she had ever heard.

CHAPTER NINE

ANNA opened her eyes to hear Dan's voice at the radio, her feeling of disbelief that she had actually been asleep for some time making her look about her with dazed eyes. She was still looking around her as Dan turned, his eyes meeting hers. They were alive, still here! Her face lit up with a smile and he came to stand over her.

'It's finished.'

He stood looking down at her, his smile reaching hers.

'I actually slept!'

'After a long time. It's morning—at least, it's first light. I've been on to Nassau. The hurricane just clipped us. We didn't get a direct hit, after all.'

'Will it come back?'

'No. They feed on water. It's hit the eastern coast of the States. It will blow itself out.' He reached for her hand. 'Want to see the damage?'

He pulled her to her feet, his arms catching her as she swayed.

'Have you been out?'

'A few yards. The radio dragged me back, but I couldn't get to it before you began to stir.'

He went on holding her, and she was still too hazy to move. She may only have slept for a little while, but she had slept deeply. She felt warm, secure, an almost feline pleasure in her body. He didn't say a word. The smiling eyes held her as fast as his arms held her, and she had no thought of moving from him.

'So you came back?'

'Yes.' It was only a murmured agreement, and she had not had any difficulty in following his chain of thought.

'I sent you away.'

'I had to see you!'

He just nodded, his face warm and understanding. His eyes began to search her face, the slender length of her neck and the pulse that began to beat rapidly where the soft shirt buttoned. His gaze rested on the upward tilt of her breasts, mounds of pleasure, straining beneath the white covering of cotton.

Steadily his hands moved from her shoulder to sweep in one breathtaking caress from her breast to her thigh, and he pulled her close until her hips were against his.

His head swooped down, and the warmth of his mouth covered hers in a lingering kiss that was almost tender, his lips moving over hers gently, softly.

'Let's look at the storm damage,' he murmured, his head lifting at last. He turned her to the door, his arm still around her waist, and she knew that all at once everything was different. His lips had told her. The quiet of his voice had told her. The strong, possessive caress had been his unspoken admission.

The interior of the house looked just the same, nothing broken or lost. But as Anna stepped through the front door into a grey and watery dawn she was thankful they had only caught the edge of the hurricane. The sea looked sullen and grey, seaweed and sediment dispelling the lovely colour she was accustomed to. And the island had been brutalised!

The small quay was wrecked, its strong planks so much flotsam, much of it not there at all, the wreckage floating

in the sea. Not one plant had survived in the garden, the beautiful hibiscus gone as if it had never been, and much of the lawn had been raked bare.

The beach was strewn with the battered remains of the beautiful palms, and, although many of them still stood, some of them were snapped like matchwood, and others had been stripped of their bark. Branches and twigs had been driven into the window shutters like arrows, and Anna could see what would have happened had Dan not taken precautions. Yet this had merely been a near miss, the edge of the danger.

'What damage to the house?' she asked huskily, over-whelmed by the evidence of nature's majestic fury.

'A few panes of glass and a few tiles,' he said with satisfaction. 'Not bad at all.'

'What about the launch?'

'Ah! That's something yet again. I'll take down the shutters and then I'll go over there and see what happened.'

His arm left her waist and his mind left hers; the house, the launch and Amara Cay were now his immediate concern.

Anna went inside and started to clear up. The first job was to make everything look as it had done. That seemed terribly important, because Dan loved it all and so did she. The pictures were heavy, but she struggled and somehow managed to get them back into place, re-membering with love each special spot, wanting things to look right before Dan came back. The ornaments she handled with tender care. They were wonderful, each piece chosen as if it meant something. She had loved them on sight. She stood back and surveyed her work, well-satisfied, and then she tackled the kitchen.

She was just washing last night's dishes when Dan came in, wet to the waist and muddy.

'Is the launch still there?' She swung round and looked at him, her eyes opening in surprise at his dishevelled appearance, and he nodded, that slow smile growing again.

'A bit battered but the bay is sheltered. I left it there as there's no place to tie up here at the moment. The journey through to it is hazardous. Don't go wandering. Some of the trees are going to come down.'

He glanced at the dishes.

'No more water. We may run short until things sort themselves out!'

'Oh, I wanted a shower.'

'Me first, I think!' Dan said with a laugh, glancing down at his own unkempt looks. 'If there's any water left you can have a quick shower next, but take it easy on everything until I tell you otherwise.'

He went towards his room and she dried the dishes and put them away, just finishing when he called that she could now use her ration of water.

She felt as if she had been sleeping in her clothes for a whole week, and she pulled them off as she went towards the shower in her room, letting them stay as they fell. It reminded her of Anita and Josie's complaints, but she pushed the past and the future out of her mind. She was stiff and tired, but she knew that even today Dan could not force her to go. Even if a boat came in, there was nowhere to tie up. He was hers for one more day, and his kiss had acknowledged it. They had shared the terrifying night, faced things together. She would remember it always.

She was careful, soaping herself and then showering, trying not to waste the precious water, but her mind was only half on the task. Somewhere inside her was a growing elation, an expectation, excitement welling up like a clear, bubbling stream as the water cascaded down her black hair. She was conscious of the pleasure of the water on her skin, her body alive with awareness, a breathless waiting inside her.

A slight noise made her turn her head, but she felt no surprise. Dan was standing there, his brown body covered by a short black robe, his tawny eyes alight as they moved over her. His vibrant gaze moved from the glistening length of her black hair to the rounded swell of her breasts and down the slender length of her legs, his eyes moving back to devour her over again.

She felt no shyness, no desire to hide or cover the shimmering body that his eyes embraced. She just looked at him, her breathing shallow, her pulse rapid, and he came forward slowly, his eyes on hers as he discarded his robe and stepped under the water, his arms closing around her as she moved willingly to him.

She wound her arms around his neck and his hands moved over her wet skin, shaping her waist and the slender length of her thighs.

'You knew I would come,' he murmured against her face.

'Yes!' She moved against him and gasped, his arms tightening.

'How did you know?' he asked thickly.

'I wanted you to come so very much.'

'Witch!' His lips searched her cheeks and the line of her neck. 'Kiss me.' It was a mere whisper again, the words spoken on a husky breath, the words she had

longed to hear, and she searched for his lips with a blind passion, the same passion for Dan that dictated all her movements, all her thoughts.

'Anna! Anna!' His lips captured hers, deepening the soft kisses with a powerful urgency as she wound herself around him, her wet body sinuous and warm, like a gift from the sea.

They didn't speak. Desperation was in all their movements, their hearts thundering together. The kisses were wild, deep, fired by necessity, the precious water forgotten as it rained down on them, his body closely entwined with her own.

'I need you!' He gasped out the words and lifted her closer. He seemed to be possessed of superhuman strength as he held her against him, parting her thighs, driven to take her with no ability to wait, and she clung to him willingly, her lips fused with his.

Fire shot through her as she arched against him, a moan of passion deep in her throat, her body moving with the fierce rhythm of his possession until he lowered her to her feet, her body lethargic in the aftermath of his frenzied demands.

She was hardly aware that he turned off the water, that he moved and tied a towel around her waist. Even as he lifted her out and stood her on the soft carpet, her heavy lids would scarcely lift more than a little way. He wrapped her long hair in a towel, enclosing her in another and lifting her into his arms.

She felt the bed beneath her but the world had gone, nothing existed any more but the face that hovered over her, the brown fingers that traced her cheeks.

'Dan!' It was the slightest sound, a faint murmur that seemed to come from a very long way off, but he would not allow even that.

'Shh!' He unwrapped her long hair, his hands against her trembling skin as he moved the other towel that covered her. 'Don't speak, sweet Anna! Don't say anything at all,' he breathed. 'I needed you fiercely, but now I'm going to love you.'

He had taken her almost ferociously, like a man driven to desperation, but now his touch was gentle, his lips searching her body as his hands had done before. Every skilful caress drew her back to life, his reassuring murmurs breathed against her skin as she moaned in delight. His mouth moved back to hers, his tongue stroking her lips before moving down to stroke against the tight, rosy peaks of her breasts.

'Dan!' The ecstasy became too much for her to bear, her voice pleaded, and his body, hard and strong, came back to her, compelling a further surrender, his possession tender until she cried aloud for satisfaction and he crushed her against him with the same urgency he had shown before.

She was trembling uncontrollably as she spiralled back to earth, her eyes deep and dark on his face, awe and wonder in their black depths, and he watched her for one long moment before tossing the towels to the floor and pulling her back into his arms, covering them with the cool sheets.

'You're tired,' he said softly, his fingers tracing her tremulous lips.

'Yes.' She was languid, wondering why she couldn't speak, why his eyes seemed to fill the whole world. 'Yes, I'm tired.'

'Then sleep with me, darling.'

. The word rang through her brain like a crystal bell, and she turned her head to his shoulder as her eyes closed. This was not what her mind had imagined for so long. This was a heaven, a belonging she had never known.

'Dan!' She whispered his name and he seemed to understand without further words. His arms enclosed her in safety and she slept.

It was almost noon before Anna awoke, and Dan was not there. The sheets were twisted around her waist and she felt a ridiculous burst of anxiety that he should have seen her like this. She would not let her mind think of what had happened. He had sent her away and she had come back. She had slept with Dan because she had wanted to. How did he feel now, in the bright light of day?

Her clothes were where she had dropped them, and she picked them up, folding them slowly before going to see if there was any water left. There was, and she used it sparingly before dressing in the only other clothes she had; the white dress she had arrived in. Even so, she lingered. Here in this room was the memory of happiness, more than happiness. She realised that she was afraid to leave it behind and step into the day.

There was breakfast on the table as she went into the kitchen—a very late breakfast—but Dan was not there, although the coffee was hot and newly made. She heard the sound of an approaching boat, and soon found out why he had suddenly abandoned his task. Someone was coming to the island on a fast, powerful launch that was even now slowing.

The open door drew her reluctantly. At this moment it would have been good if she was here alone with Dan. She had no idea what was in his mind. He had hardly spoken at all as they had made love, and nothing had changed. He still had one life here, she another. Here in the house where she had stayed with Dan, the hours they had spent locked in each other's arms seemed unreal.

It was a police launch, and any lingering magic died as Anna saw who was standing on deck, waving frantically to Dan. She remembered only too well the fair hair, the beautiful face. Daphne was coming home, and Dan was waiting for her, his face alive with happiness.

The boat was brought close in and one of the policemen climbed out to the shredded remains of the little quay, his arms reaching for Daphne, and then passing her to Dan. She linked her arms around his neck, laughing up into his face as he took her and brought her safely to dry land. They were both so joyful. There was a look of contentment about Dan that she could see even from here. Anna turned and went inside before they saw her, but there was nowhere to hide. The launch waited a few minutes, Dan talking to the men on board, and then it veered away from the island. She had to face whatever was coming.

She was back in the kitchen when they came in, her unsteady hands pouring coffee, and she made herself look up with a smile. It was the hardest thing she had ever had to do in her life.

'Why, it's Anna! I'll never forget that exotic colouring! I had no idea you were here. You faced the storm?'

'Yes. It was an experience!' Anna half smiled, stiffening as Dan walked into the room. She didn't want to

look at him reproachfully. She didn't feel reproachful. She understood.

His eyes came instantly to her face, his smile dying as he saw her tight restraint, and he took the coffee she handed to him without looking at her further.

'Now, you've got some explaining to do!'

He leaned against the table and smiled across at Daphne, his whole attitude indulgent and at ease. It was so very obvious that they were close, involved with each other, and Anna felt a burst of shame as she realised that had she been in Daphne's place she would not have been greeting another woman so warmly, not when that other woman had been alone with Dan. Of course, Daphne remembered her as a little-sister figure and not in any way as a threat. She was no threat, she could see that.

'It's a flying visit only.' Daphne laughed. 'That launch is picking me up in about one hour. They're skimming round the Out Islands to check up on people, and then they're coming back for me. I mentioned your name and they obliged quickly.'

'Johnny's a friend of mine, and in any case, they try to oblige after anything like this,' Dan said. 'It still doesn't explain the visit.'

'I was on my way here to see you when the hurricane warning went out. As soon as it was over I simply continued. I had to find out how you were, Dan. After all, I've got a vested interest in you!' She laughed in a low amused way, her eyes rueful. 'It's also the little matter of Anita.'

'Ah! We'll leave that standing right there for now. And how is Trevor?' Dan asked with a wide grin.

Anna didn't want to hear any more. Dan had not even looked at her after that quick glance when he had come in. She waited until there was a break in the conversation, and then got ready to add her own part. She never got the chance; Dan said it for her.

'We'll go across on the launch when it comes back, Anna,' he said, his eyes glancing across at her. 'The water isn't going to last and the whole island needs some work done on it. I'll see to you and then find Abe. He can bring a work gang out here. When you've eaten, you can get your things together ready to leave.'

She just nodded numbly. One more day was all she had asked for, and one more day was all he was offering. He had made his position quite clear when she had been in hospital, and he had not changed his mind. She couldn't eat. She quickly swallowed her coffee and left them alone.

'She's astonishingly beautiful, Dan.' Daphne's voice drifted to her as she went to her room. 'That hair, those dark eyes . . .'

'Yes, she's beautiful!' There was a harsh sound to Dan's voice, a deep-lying anger that he tried to contain, and she didn't linger. She could hear them talking rapidly though, even from her room; they were so accustomed to each other, with so much to say. She dared not go back in case she found Daphne in Dan's arms, because she couldn't stand that.

In the end, after a long time, Dan came to find her.

'What are you doing?' He just walked in on her as if it was a very natural thing to do, and it almost amused her to realise that he only sounded intrigued.

'Just pottering about. I thought I'd leave you to catch up on your news.'

'There's not much news,' he said with a quizzical look at her. 'I do hear from Daphne regularly. We keep in close touch. We have to.'

It might have been the understatement of the year! Naturally they kept in close touch, with a son to share!

'I understand that.' She looked away, her eyes downcast.

'I'd like it if you looked at me,' Dan told her softly, coming across the room to her. 'I wanted to talk to you when I got up, but you looked so deeply asleep, so comfortable, that I left you there.'

She remembered how she had looked, and her face flushed rosily.

'Hey!' His hand tilted her face. 'Why this shyness? It's a pity that there's no time left, or I would have to get you out of this mood.' His lips brushed her cheeks.

She knew there was no time left and she wasn't going to beg to stay with him.

'You don't need to talk to me, Dan,' she said quickly, forcing herself to meet his intrigued eyes. 'I understand everything you want to say.'

'Do you?' He took her slender shoulders in his hands and looked down at her, but Daphne called from the hall.

'Time's up, Dan! The launch is coming. I can hear it!'

He still stood looking down at Anna, his smile only very tentative.

'I'll never understand you,' he said softly. 'You always were such a strange little creature, watching from the shadows.'

'Dan!' Daphne's voice was more urgent. 'Time's up! I have a plane to catch.'

'Coming!' He turned and walked out. 'Hurry up, Anna,' he said almost wearily. 'If we miss this lift then you're going to be stranded here until Abe decides to risk a trip out.'

And he didn't want her stranded here. She had a plane to catch, too. It wouldn't take her long. Everything was already at the airport. Dan wouldn't have to arrange it again.

They went out the way that Daphne had come in, Dan lifting them both and handing them to one of the men on the launch. As he lifted her, his arms tightened around her momentarily, but she was stiff and unyielding, protecting herself from all feeling, and as he leapt on to the launch his face was as stiff and tight as she felt.

He didn't have anything to say to her—he didn't get the chance, for Daphne talked non-stop, shouting over the roar of the engines. Anna watched her animated face. She was different from the woman who had come with Dan to Langford Hall almost five years ago. The unhappiness, the vulnerability had gone. Life was good to her, Anna could tell that. She turned away from them and watched for the first sign of Nassau, the end of her dreams, escape.

Daphne wasn't lingering. Apparently she had spent more time waiting out the hurricane than she had allowed for, and she said goodbye to Anna pleasantly.

'It was a very short visit,' Anna said, more for something to say than anything else, her heart astounded that she still liked this woman.

'Well, I was half-way here. I thought I may as well come right on. I can't spend much time away from Trevor, but I can't go too long without seeing Dan.'

Their way of living astonished Anna. She couldn't go any time at all without seeing Dan; she never had been able to all her life. From now on, though, she would never see him again. She just allowed herself to be led to a taxi, her arm lifeless in Dan's firm grip, and they both saw Daphne into another taxi. Anna closed her eyes as Dan kissed Daphne goodbye.

She wasn't really aware of where they were going until the taxi stopped at a hotel and Dan lifted out his luggage and her own small case.

'Now,' he said tersely as he marched her inside, 'you and I have some talking to do!'

He was angry, his voice quite harsh as he booked two rooms. There was plenty of room. Most of the tourists had fled, one of them on her own seat on the plane, she realised that now. He would be leaving her here until he found her another place on a flight to England. She followed him into the lift and stood silently by as he opened a door and ushered her inside.

'Your room,' he assured her testily. 'I'm next door. As you haven't eaten a thing since last night, I'll order you something now, then I'll find Abe and after that I'll get around to you!'

He was angry with her for coming back, for complicating his life, angry with himself for making love to her. She didn't blame him; after all, hadn't she thrown herself at Dan since she had been here? Perhaps things would have been different if Daphne had not suddenly appeared, but it would only have been for one more day.

She said nothing and he went to the door, walking out and leaving her without a backward glance. She gave him ten minutes and then called the desk.

'Is it possible to arrange a flight to England from here?' she asked quickly. It was, and they rang back almost at once to say that a flight left in half an hour, just time for her to make it to the airport. They even called a taxi for her. It was very easy to leave the Bahamas.

She looked all right. This dress was still fresh. She hadn't worn it except for the little time of getting to Amara Cay and the time before she had changed. Her luggage was already at the airport. Dan was going to come back and tell her all about Daphne, say he was sorry, and she couldn't listen to that.

CHAPTER TEN

THERE was no frantic bustle at the airport now, and checking her luggage in was a simple matter. Everything was back to normal, the sky clear and blue as it had been on the day she arrived. Food would be served once they were airborne, but even then she would not be able to eat. The emptiness inside was not because she was hungry. She was filled with desolation and loneliness.

Her flight was called and she walked forward almost blindly, seeing nothing but the bleak future; nothing to dream of, nothing to hope for. Her head was down and she hardly knew where she went, her weary steps simply following other passengers.

'Where the hell do you think you're going?'

Dan's furious voice brought her back to the present with a heart-jerking snap, his hand on her arm like steel. She turned quickly and he was beside her, his face harsh and flushed with anger. He looked incapable of keeping any sort of self-control, and there was a violence about him that sent a shiver of fear through her.

She could only stand and stare at him, shaking her head numbly. She was going home, back to the place she belonged, saving him the embarrassment of telling her yet again to leave. What was all this anger about? Perhaps she should have waited to say goodbye, but she could not have done that. Many times in her life she had said goodbye to Dan, but this time she had been incapable of it.

'My flight's been called!'

It was all she could think to say and he actually shook her, his eyes blazing with rage, a low animal sound of danger deep in his throat.

His towering rage was drawing attention to them, and she looked anxiously round, keeping her voice low.

'You know I have to go, Dan! You can surely understand?'

'Understand what? Understand that you came back to me, slept with me, and now you're regretting it and going off to that over-worked, half-baked doctor? No, I don't understand!'

He was shouting, utterly uncaring whether anyone heard or not, a white line of fury around his mouth. And they did hear. Without even looking, Anna was aware that they were the focus of many interested eyes, and her colour mounted rapidly.

'Dan, please!' She tried to pull away, but he only gripped her tighter.

'Can I help you, miss?' A man who seemed to be suicidal came forward, and Dan turned on him like a tiger, his powerful body tensed like an animal disturbed at the kill.

'Yes, you can help! Mind your own damned business!'

'It's all right, thank you,' Anna said quickly. Dan had had enough, he almost dragged her away from the barrier.

'My luggage! It's on the flight!'

'Surely you deserve some inconvenience?' he snarled. 'You've been inconveniencing me all my life!'

'Not any more!'

She pulled at his hand, some measure of spirit returning to her dulled brain, but he looked at her in a truly menacing way.

'I can lead you out or I can carry you out. It's all one to me!'

She went with him, every eye present following their progress.

'Can you...' She turned frantic eyes on the people at the desk.

'Get your luggage off the flight? I'll try!' The amusement in the woman's voice merely heightened Anna's colour, but she didn't have to face any more amused looks. Dan almost dragged her out, leaving people to think whatever they chose. His anger was a burning, primitive thing, bubbling close to the surface.

There was a taxi waiting, its engine running, and Dan pushed her inside, his hand never leaving her arm, sure in his own mind apparently that she would open the opposite door and run.

'You got her, Mr Toren?'

A grinning black face looked at her through the rear mirror, and Dan growled irritably, 'I got her! Take us back to the hotel.'

There was nothing to say, and in any case she dared not. Dan was almost raging, out of control. What did he expect of her? Did he want her to stay and fill his time whenever he was away from Daphne? Did he really imagine she was running back to Bryan, or was that merely an excuse? He had held her all night, made love to her! What sort of person did he think she was, anyway?

'How did you know that...?'

'You booked your flight through the hotel! You're not as clever as you imagine.'

Some of her misery was swamped by a rising temper of her own, but she would not make a spectacle of herself in front of the self-satisfied driver of this taxi. He had

them back to the hotel swiftly, and Dan held her arm in the same tight grip as he paid the fare.

'Thanks. You made it just in time!'

He gave the man a whole wad of notes, and the man let out a whoop of delight that drew further attention to them, but their passage through the foyer of the hotel was too swift for any other would-be spectators to get more than a glimpse of a dangerously angry man with thick hair of bronzed gold, and a girl with tight lips and long black hair that almost reached her waist.

'Now——'

Dan almost flung her into her room, locking the door and pocketing the key. He stood watching her as she walked quickly away, putting some distance between them.

'You'd better explain to me why you were taking off like that, without a word, with no thought for me!' he grated, his eyes narrowed and dangerous. 'If you imagine that I'm allowing you to erase your fixation with me in one brief spell of passion and then slip off back to the boyfriend, then you've never been more mistaken!'

She whirled round in astonishment, stunned by his words.

'I asked for everything I got! Is that what you're telling me? Because don't bother, I know! I begged for one more day. Well, it's over!'

'And what about me?' His voice was heavy with bitterness, quieter, the rage subsiding a little as another emotion took its place.

'There's Daphne,' she reminded him quietly, and he turned away, his hand running distractedly through his hair.

'God give me strength! Is this because Daphne arrived? I told you, I'm not married to Daphne. Don't you believe that?'

'Yes, I believe it. It doesn't make any difference nowadays though, does it—marriage? Then there's your son and...'

'What son?' He turned on her with almost wild eyes. 'You get more odd every day, do you know that? You've invented a son for me now? There *is* no son!'

'Trevor...' she began shakily, her world upside-down, five years of beliefs juddering ready to fall.

'Trevor is not mine. He's Daphne's! Let's hear any more crimes that I've committed.'

'It doesn't matter,' she said with weary patience. 'You wanted me to go. You told me to go. You even got my ticket.'

'Only because you begged not to come back to Amara Cay.'

He strode over to her, looking at her frustratedly.

'All the time I was getting you to hospital, all the time I was sitting beside you praying for that fever to break, you rambled on. You never wanted to go back to Amara, never, never, never!'

He grasped her shoulders, jerking her forward, hard against his chest, a reckless look about him that held her still.

'I love you! Sending you away almost killed me. When you came back, I couldn't believe it!' He let her go and turned away, his shoulders suddenly defeated. 'You *did* want to go, didn't you? What am I, after all, but a long-time obsession that's now exorcised?'

She stood like stone. Her ears heard, but her heart refused to believe. Her whole life seemed to have been one of waiting, longing for Dan in some way, and now

he was behaving as if *he* was lost, lonely. His unhappiness was too real to mistake.

'You can go if you want to, Anna,' he said bitterly, his head turned away, his eyes on the blue sky through the window. 'I've survived for almost five years without you, what's the rest of my miserable life?'

She said nothing because words wouldn't come, and when he turned to look at her, tears were streaming down her face, her trembling hands held out to him.

'Oh, Dan, I love you so much! There's nothing in my life when you're not there, there never has been! Don't say you love me if you don't mean it. I couldn't bear that!'

For one second he looked at her in disbelief, and then he reached for her, pulling her into his arms, his face against her wet cheeks.

'Anna! My Anna! Surely you know I love you?'

He rocked her against him, his lips searching her face, closing her eyes. His hands twisted into her long hair and he held her fast, looking at her for a long time.

'Darling, there's nobody else,' he said quietly. He took a deep breath, almost like a sigh. 'There's been nobody else for over four years, ever since I found you. I've buried myself on Amara, trying to make it beautiful, gathering things you would love, hoping that one day you'd come to me.'

'You bought Amara because of me?'

It was too soon, too much. Her mind dared not take this all in and believe it.

'I bought Amara so that I could have some peace. I wanted to build a dream place, a place to bring you, somewhere that was just for the two of us. Not many people are welcome on Amara Cay.'

'Daphne is,' she said tensely. 'And the woman who owns the wetsuit.'

'You don't trust me.' His voice returned to bitterness, and he started to move away, his hands rejecting her.

'Don't leave me!' She clung to him frantically, crushing the last shreds of jealousy. 'I've trusted you all my life! If I hadn't, I would never have—have . . .'

'Given yourself to me so sweetly, so wildly?' he finished for her, hauling her back into his arms. 'Daphne is a friend, and I hope that you'll have her for a friend too, if only for my sake. The lady with the wetsuit brings her husband.' He looked down at her with such love that she couldn't doubt him ever. 'I love *you*!' he said huskily. He raised her hand to his lips, kissing the warmth of her palm.

'Oh, Dan, why didn't you come for me? I thought you were going to marry Daphne! You said so.'

'How could I come? I hurt you so much, and I knew it. I was locked in a whirl of my own guilt, and you were only seventeen. I imagined you were over it. When I came to the wedding and saw how you greeted your doctor, I was sure of that!'

'As if I could be!' She looked up at him with dark eyes, and he sank to a chair, taking her with him.

'I'd better tell you about Daphne,' he sighed. 'You're going to listen to me, Anna, because there must never be any misunderstanding between us again, nothing to separate us!'

'There couldn't be!' She curled up against him and he laughed shakily.

'I'm not taking the risk! I know you of old. You've been elusive all your life!'

Not really, she thought, only too committed to one person, too afraid to show it. Now she could let him

know. Now all her love could be poured on to Dan. She rested her head against his shoulder, listening blissfully to the deep sound of his voice.

'Tell me about Daphne,' she said softly, and his arms tightened around her.

'I've known her for years. When I first came over to write the screenplay for a book, I had really no idea how to go about it. Daphne is a screenwriter and she worked with me. I got to know her well and I got to know Trevor Blaine, her fiancé. They were the best friends I had.'

He was silent for a minute, and she knew that this was painful to him.

'You don't have to tell me.' Her hand stroked his face and he captured it, bring it back to his lips.

'I need to. No more secrets, no more ghosts. Trevor was a stunt man,' he continued, his voice low. 'And you know what my books are like—political thrillers, fast and furious, plenty of scope for a stunt man. It's all very well to write these things, but somehow different to get them on to film. Nearly five years ago we came to a really sticky patch in the book that was being filmed. It needed a spectacular accident, and it was important to the story, not just a gimmick. Dean looked at it and said it would have to go. He wanted something else written in. I agreed, but with a great deal of reluctance. Trevor was all for keeping it. He thought it through and said he could do it. He also said it would be the best thing he had ever done, and it would push him right to the top. He even got me enthusiastic, and we overruled Dean. In fact, we haunted him until he gave in.'

Dan sighed, his face resting in her hair.

'I don't know what went wrong. Perhaps Trevor was over-confident, perhaps he prepared a bit carelessly, perhaps he lost his concentration, or maybe it was just

impossible. He crashed. When they got to him, he was dead.'

'And you felt completely responsible,' she said softly, her slender arms winding around him.

'Yes. Daphne was sedated and in hospital for almost a week, and I went every day. I was filled with guilt. I felt that it was all down to me. I should have just said no and written it out.'

'When she finally began to talk, she could only talk to me, and she told me she was pregnant. I asked her to marry me and she just looked at me blankly, but I went on and told her that she needed someone to take care of her, to help bring up Trevor's baby. It wasn't going to be any sort of marriage, we didn't even need to discuss that. We were just friends, and finally she said yes. The ring you saw was Trevor's. It never left her finger and I knew it never would.

'Everyone who was close to us knew all about it and they rallied round. For a long time she couldn't be left alone, and when I came to England, I brought her with me. That's when you saw her and when I realised that guilt had robbed me of something that had been there right under my nose for most of my life.'

'Why didn't you explain to me?'

She lifted her head and kissed him, quick, loving kisses that went some way to banish the sombre mood that had grown on him as he talked softly. He held her close.

'How could I? Daphne needed me, and you were just becoming a woman. You needed to forget me. It was a childish fixation and nothing more. I was the one with the problem.'

He tilted her face and looked into her eyes, his lips coming to touch hers.

'I used to look at you when you were a child and puzzle about what to do, what you needed,' he murmured, his eyes moving over her face longingly. 'You always looked as if you wanted me to care for you, but if I tried you acted as if I was a monster. I always went away worried about you, worried about the strange creature who had moved into our lives and who watched me with dark, wary eyes.

'Dad used to tell me about the scrapes you got into, but I could hardly believe it. When I was home you were unnaturally still, watching and waiting, secret and dark. I used to go off worried, wondering why you were so scared of me. I had this picture in my mind of a thin little girl with long black hair and dark, intelligent eyes.

'When I came home with Daphne, I just couldn't believe the change that had taken place in three years. You came out of the door to meet us and you were a woman— cool, controlled, exotically beautiful. It stunned me!'

'I wanted to cry,' she confessed. 'You brought Daphne and everything seemed to fall to pieces!'

'Darling, don't!' He drew her close and kissed her, his hand warm and possessive against her face. 'I've never wanted to hurt you in my life.' His head sank to her breast, his hands caressing her. 'You bewitched me! All that long week I couldn't see enough of you, but you were no closer to me than you had ever been. You avoided my eyes, and when I looked up unexpectedly those dark eyes were always on me, the same look in them that I remembered, wanting something that I couldn't understand. This time though you were grown up, beautiful, poignant, sitting in the shadows, like a tantalising little phantom at the edge of my world. I wanted to pull you into my world, into my life. Before

the week was out I was so much in love with you that I knew I had to go and never come back!'

'I thought it was the end of my life!' She smoothed the thick hair from his forehead and he looked up at her quizzically.

'Was it?'

'You told me that I'd recover. I did, at least my logic told me that I had. Maybe I would have recovered faster if you hadn't kissed me.'

'I didn't mean to! When you didn't come to say goodbye, I had to see you, although I knew how dangerous it was. When you cried, I wanted to take you with me, but my conscience was too strong. Daphne needed me, it was all my fault, and I'd already asked her to marry me. You had a life ahead of you. You were brilliant. You didn't need me.'

'I did!' She looked at him almost angrily, and he smiled slowly.

'I knew that when I kissed you, but it was all too late. I never thought I'd get another chance.'

'Why didn't you marry Daphne?' It was worrying her, and he had said that nothing was to be a secret any more.

'She gradually came through it. At first she wasn't in a fit state, and then she came to me and said that she could never marry anyone. Nothing would move her. I helped her through everything and we have become really close friends. Trevor's son was born and he's a wonderful little chap. Now she's met someone else and she's beginning to pick up her life again. Trevor's ring is on her other hand. I don't suppose you noticed that, witch?'

'No, I didn't. I was too busy being jealous, and feeling guilty about it because I liked her. I wondered what you were talking about. I didn't dare come back in.'

'You imagined a love scene?' He laughed down at her and then pulled a wry face. 'We were talking about Anita. Daphne's going to finish off the last bits of the script. Anita won't roll her eyes at Daphne. We were talking about you, too,' he confessed huskily. 'I told her that I loved you, that I was never going to allow you to come back to Amara in case anything happened to you.'

'You still want me to go?'

Her eyes lifted to his face, a burst of fear deepening their brilliance even now.

'I'm going with you!' he said with vibrant urgency. 'I came here today to get tickets for both of us, not just for you. You were hurt on Amara. I was terrified when you had that fever! Then there was the hurricane.'

He pulled her close, taking a ragged breath that showed he still remembered the fear when she was so ill, but she moved back, looking up into his face.

'I love Amara Cay. I thought I'd caused so much trouble, I thought there was Daphne and that little boy. I knew I could never keep away from you if I went back, so I wanted to tell you that I never would go back. I wasn't begging for release, Dan! I was promising to let you live as you wanted to.'

'Say that again,' he urged thickly, his hands warm and exciting on her skin. 'Tell me that part about not being able to keep away from me!'

'I think you know I can't,' she confessed breathlessly.

His hand moved the neck of her dress aside, exposing the golden silk of her shoulder, but it was not enough, his fingers slipped the buttons, his eyes on the beauty of her naked breast.

'Beautiful, exotic witch!' he breathed thickly. 'Show me how you can't keep away from me!'

She was already aroused by the slowly caressing hand, and his words lit the last flame. She pulled his hand to her breast as her lips opened beneath his; passion, need and excitement present in the swift arch of her body to his touch.

He released her and stood, lifting her into his arms, walking to the bed and lowering her to it, his eyes heavy with desire as he undressed her. She knelt, warm and naked before him as she removed his clothes, her lips tracing the smooth warm of his skin, delight in her at the uncontrolled clenching of strong muscles as she touched him. Her hands traced his body with the same pleasure that he was showing as he touched her, and he trembled violently, pushing her back to the soft mattress, coming to rest beside her, his tawny eyes half closed.

'Now, sea nymph,' he murmured huskily, 'tell me your secrets, speak to me with your dark eyes, prove that you want me as much as I want you!'

'I—I can't,' she whispered. 'I'm too shy. All my life I...'

'You want to come back to my island?' he murmured, his teeth gently biting her skin, his tongue circling the high peaks of her breasts.

'Yes! Oh, yes! I want to be with you. I want to live on Amara with you. I never want to go away!'

'I keep everyone away,' he teased roughly, his heart pounding against hers. 'If you want to come with me, then show me how much. Make love to me!'

Anna moved slowly, her heart taking on a pounding rhythm as she moved to look down at him. He was serious, because in spite of his teasing words there was a raw look at the back of his eyes, almost a fear, a

pleading. He needed her to prove more than an obsession, more than a child's strange fixation.

She lowered her head and began to kiss his body, only the memory of the pleasure he had given her to guide her. Her hands moved over his skin, lingering where his body shivered at her touch, her lips following her fingers, her whole being thrilling to know that he found it difficult to lie so still.

Her fingers trailed shyly over the strong length of his legs, her tongue against the salt taste of his skin, the flat strength of his stomach, moving slowly lower as his breath became a harsh rasp in his throat.

'Anna!' His hands reached for her, lifting her head, his breathing tortured as he pulled her towards him, forcing her over his heated body, moulding her against him. 'I can't take any more!'

'You told me to make love to you. Wasn't it right?' she whispered shakily.

'Right?' He could not keep the tight stillness now, his body moved restlessly beneath her, his hands urging her closer. 'It could have driven me mad, worse than I've been these years without you!'

'I wanted to show you that my obsession...'

He spun her to the bed, his body tightly over hers.

'If it's an obsession, then I'm obsessed too. It's love, darling, love as wild and deep as it can get!'

His lips fused with hers and there were no more words but words of passion, words of love, and in Anna's mind she was back on an island; but it was not Amara Cay, it was an island filled with shimmering lights that faded into velvet darkness, until she opened her eyes to see Dan's triumphant gaze upon her flushed face, the tawny eyes filled with joy.

'You're mine!' he said softly.

'And you are mine,' Anna whispered as he kissed away happy tears that filled her dark eyes.

'Take me back to Amara,' Anna begged softly as they lay close in each other's arms later.

'When I've married you,' Dan said firmly

'How long does it take here?' She looked up at him from her safe resting place against his brown shoulder, and he shook his head.

'I've no idea. I've never been married before.'

They looked at each other for a long time, and Dan smiled wickedly.

'In a minute, I'll get all the information we need by telephone, and then we'll simply wait it out—right here!'

'What about Langford Hall?' Anna asked later when she was not quite so breathless from Dan's kisses. 'What about Edna, for that matter?'

'We need two homes!' Dan said determinedly. 'I'll never let you sit out a hurricane again. We'll spend half our time here, and the other half at Langford Hall. Any unhappy memories will disappear.'

'Edna for one half of the year and Josie for the other half!' Anna laughed. 'Who could want more?'

She looked at him thoughtfully as another idea came into her mind.

'What about my degree, Dan? What am I supposed to do with a first-class honours degree in maths when I'm on Amara Cay for half the year?'

Some of the happiness faded from his face, and he turned to her seriously, a tight anxiety about him.

'You tell me,' he invited quietly. 'You had plenty of plans.'

'Well, I've never noticed a bank on Amara,' she said with a thoughtful frown that had his smile growing again, 'so that seems to be out. As to government, I intend to

be the whole government of our little kingdom, so temporarily, I'll frame my degree and hang it over the bed!'

'I love you!' Dan whispered urgently, holding her tightly. 'I'm trying not to be selfish, I'm trying not to own everything about you.' He looked at her seriously. 'You're so clever, my Anna, I don't have the right.'

'Don't worry,' she teased, 'I'll think of something to keep my brain from stagnating. I'll tell you something!' she added pertly. 'My children will be the smartest children you've ever met!'

'And every last one of them called Toren,' Dan said contentedly.

In the end they were married in England. They both wanted to share their happiness with Elaine, and Dan had another reason.

'When Elaine got married,' he said softly, 'I looked at you as you walked behind her and I said to myself, "One day, my love, you'll walk down this aisle, but you'll be walking in front and you'll be walking to me." Now it's all come true. I want to see it happen. I want to turn round in that same church with the same people and watch you walk to me, right out of the edge of my life into the centre of it.'

'I tried to keep out of your way,' Anna murmured from the safety of his arms.

'Why?'

'I had to fight the feelings that still hurt, but when I was at Oxford and you told me you were going back to the island, I felt so lonely.' She looked up at him, her hand against the silken rasp of his face. 'Why didn't you go?'

'I never had any intention of going without you,' he said with a smile. 'You didn't want me there, but I

couldn't leave you. It was my turn to step into the shadows and wait.'

'What if I hadn't made myself ill with work and that cold?'

'I would still have been waiting,' he assured her deeply. 'I'm glad that I didn't have to, but I would have been at Langford Hall or some other place, just waiting for as long as it took.'

'I can hardly believe that this is all true,' Anna sighed. 'I'm afraid sometimes that I'll wake up and not find your arms around me, that I dreamed it all.'

'When you have another ring behind this one,' Dan murmured, kissing her fingers, 'you'll believe it.'

He looked deeply into her eyes, love and joy burning in his own.

'I glory in having you, my Anna. You're every dream come true!'

The same look was in Anna's eyes before he closed them with tender kisses. And two weeks later, as Dan's launch, repaired and newly painted, coasted in to Amara Cay, Anna turned to him with a happy, confident laugh.

'Abe has seen to everything!' she said delightedly 'It looks just as it looked when I first came here!'

'Except then, you didn't know that it was all for you, that you belonged here with me,' Dan reminded her, lifting her to the small new quay. 'Do you know now, darling?'

'Yes, I know!'

The dark eyes flashed with happiness, every last wistful look gone, and he swung her up into his arms as Josie came to the door, her face wreathed with smiles to welcome Anna home.

Harlequin Presents

Coming Next Month

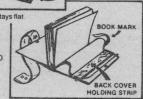

PATRICIA WILSON used to live in Yorkshire, England, but with her children all grown up, she decided to give up her teaching position there and accompany her husband on a extended trip to Spain. Their travels are providing her with plenty of inspiration for her romance writing.

Books by Patricia Wilson

"My finge[rs]
she com[e]

"Lick them," Dan murmured. Before she could move he had her hand in his, lifting her slender fingers to his lips.

"Don't!" Anna's whole body leaped as if she had been touched by an electrical charge, and she snatched her hand away.

"Merely trying to oblige," he assured her softly, taking her arm and leading her off to the boat as if nothing at all had happened.

Maybe it hadn't, for him! For her, it was just one more step along the way, one more thing to fire her wild obsession with him.

It was becoming more difficult to be natural, and often she thought that he was deliberately forcing the tension up. It was a thrill that ran through the days, a force that was dragging her under.